Close Your
EYES

Lauren
Summer 2022

Close Your
EYES

A FAIRY TALE

Chris Tomasini

Contents

PART THREE

PROLOGUE

In the early morning hours of June 1, 1431, the castle of Gora echoed and sounded with the cries of mobilizing soldiers. Preceded by hundreds of horsemen, the soldiers rumbled through the city and fanned into the surrounding countryside. The city populace awoke to the confusion, and meeting in the dark streets, neighbours questioned each other as to the reason for the hysteria. The most widely believed rumour was that forces of the Holy Roman Empire were preparing to attack our King. This caused considerable alarm, for our land had been at peace for nearly two decades, and war was thought of as a terrible plague that existed only in distant, foreign lands.

It was not war which had sent torches blazing and soldiers careening through the night, and though the true reason was known, and often spoken, it was as often dismissed, seeming too inconsequential and unlikely to be the cause of such a disturbance. The truth, which none of those people milling about in the city streets believed, was that the King's cook and storyteller had fled the castle.

I was found wandering about the castle halls that night, and a party of guards subsequently escorted me to my room. They closed me in and set two watchmen outside the door. Alone in my cell I opened the shutters of my window, leant against the stone wall, stared up at the full moon, and listened to the shouts and cries drifting from the fields and through the city. I knew that I would be unable to sleep, but nevertheless I climbed into bed where I found, to my surprise, a scroll lying hidden amongst the furs and cushions. I sat up in the darkness and held it reverently in my hands. I knew immediately what it was – my parting gift from the storyteller, from my friend Tycho.

It is now 1435. When I found Tycho's scroll in 1431 I was illiterate, and it has taken me four arduous years to learn the mysteries of the written word. Reading Tycho's scroll, which proved to be an infrequently kept journal, and certain other documents which came into my possession, I developed a desire to write the story of my friend, a daunting task, for it is the story of a storyteller.

I spoke to an old and wise friend of my desire to write Tycho's history. I asked him where I should begin, and he replied "At the beginning." I pondered this for a few days, then returned to him and asked "Which one?" The old man smiled patiently, answering "My friend, the answer lies within yourself."

That was a year ago. This business of writing, it is like being cast into a blackened dungeon, with your arms bound behind your back, and then ordered to sound out the dimensions of the room by bashing your head against the walls.

A year, but after so many false starts and counterfeit revelations, I think I have finally understood what my old friend meant.

PART ONE

1

THE ANSWER LIES WITHIN

My name is Samuel. In Cologne, in 1399, I was born a dwarf to normally sized parents. I have a brother, a year older than I, who is of normal stature as well.

At a very early age I realized that my height, or lack thereof, set me apart from the rest of the world. I won't list the disadvantages of being a dwarf, or record the cruelties I suffered at the hands of other children, but there was an advantage to my shortened frame and bow legged walk – humour. I could tell the most mundane jokes and still raise enthusiastic responses simply because my appearance added to the merriment. When I began doing physical turns – pratfalls, cartwheels, juggling, simply falling upon my face – people clapped and roared as though I were the most celebrated performer at a gypsy circus.

At thirteen years of age I weighed my few options and resigned myself to the life of a jester. I envisioned myself entertaining a just King and a beautiful Queen at a splendorous court, and when I kissed my parents goodbye and left home, I did so with a strangely light heart. I did not know where I was bound, or how to obtain a position as a court jester, but I was young, swelled by notions of life in an Arthurian Camelot, and it would be years yet before I was struck by the great sadness of my later life.

I travelled widely through the western and central parts of Christendom. I juggled on streets, did brief exhibitions in town markets, and found to my frustration that it was virtually impossible for a wandering clown to be granted an interview with a King. Failing to find employment as a court jester I simply wandered. Eventually I found myself in Oder with a partner. He was a seven foot, pale, wildly eccentric man with a jutting chin and odd, protruding, insect like eyes. We called ourselves "High and Low", and for a few brief years we were the most desired clowns in German Christendom.

I grew to hate that man, whose name was Troyden, but I can't deny our success. We became so popular that our reputation preceded us to neighbouring towns. When we arrived in some dusky village we would find a stage already hammered together, decorated with banners, awaiting our performance. We would perform night after night until we had exhausted our repertoire, and then we left, travelling clowns with the known world before us.

The roads and paths of Christendom are not for the faint of heart, and the life we led was a perilous one. We were often hungry, often lost, and we rarely knew where we would make our bed the next night. Once or twice a month we were stopped by highwaymen, but we developed a routine to deal with this. In our repertoire was a sketch where we played brain dead dolts, an incredibly tall and abnormally short one, playing chess, arguing over the rules, which we formulated as we played. When confronted by thieves we lapsed into this pretension of idiocy. We were greatly abused but took advantage of our assailants' hilarity to pick their pockets.

When these encounters finished we invariably gained more gold and silver than we lost.

Troyden and I, making our way through those forests and villages, across rivers, through snow covered fields, argued constantly. We bickered over food, meals, responsibilities, money, our act, and our arguing became another routine. On stage one night a genuine, and bitter, argument erupted between us. The crowd roared – a short and a tall man quarrelling, viciously, they could not contain themselves. It gave both of us a newfound disrespect for our audiences – people were delighted at such trivial things.

In 1415 we arrived in Gora. Fortune favoured us, giving us the chance to entertain the King and Queen after their dinner, and they adored us. King Pawel asked if it was possible that we remain in Gora indefinitely. Troyden tottered on his bony heels and had to be assisted to a chair, while I stared in amazement at the immense man before me – the most famous King in Christendom, extending us an invitation to live at perhaps the most wondrous court north of the Alps, and we barely better than glorified beggars! Of course it was possible.

But we realized, as the weeks passed, that the positions we had been given were not what we had expected. We seldom entertained the court, rather we worked almost exclusively for the King's children, Princess Alexandra, born in 1414, and Prince Krysztoff, born in 1417. Pawel was fiercely dedicated to his children, and despite all his duties as a King, his duties as a father and a husband were always preeminent.

Pawel believed that his children were the most important people in the Kingdom. He believed that assuring their happiness was the duty of his final years. To this end, amongst all the other wonders he gave them, he secured for them the most talented educators, cooks, entertainers, storytellers, tailors, riding instructors – the most talented people in every field, that could be found.

In 1415 Troyden and I became Princess Alexandra's personal clowns. When I recall that time it strikes me as a foolish endeavor – a baby lying in her small bed, absolutely oblivious to the two men dancing and acting and playing for her benefit. I was content, but as the years passed, as life at the castle both changed and remained tediously the same, Troyden, who had become very conceited about what he termed his "craft", decided that entertaining infants was below him. He told me he was leaving. I reminded him of the wolves and villains and plagues of Christendom and told him he was an imbecile. He flashed a disdainful look at me, tossed his scarf over his shoulder, and turning on his heel said "Well, say adieu to Mr. Imbecile!"

I smile now to remember these, his parting words. They are so dreadful. Troyden was a genius upon a stage, but in daily life he was the most asinine dullard I've ever known.

Troyden left and I remained. I was a teenager and the private clown for the children of King Pawel of Gora. I had found the position which I had dreamed of when I had left my home.

1435

Princess Alexandra, who is now 21 years old, has just returned to me the opening pages of my history, which I asked her to read. She approves. She laments my spelling and my atrocities to the Latin grammar, but on the whole she approves.

After bringing certain mistakes to my attention, she set a question ringing in my mind. She said "Samuel, you must imagine that your history will lie hidden in a vault, for decades, and that one day, long after you have passed from this world, perhaps when Gora itself is but a legend, your history will be unraveled by a young scholar who knows not of the places and people you describe. You must tell that scholar why this story is important – why you dedicated many long winter nights to its telling."

Why shall I, or did I, dedicate myself to the telling of this story? This sounds oddly like something Ahab once said to me. Ahab was the court astronomer, and the friend who advised me to start this history at the beginning. He once told me that a story has never been told which was not truly about its teller.

Alexandra and Ahab, both of whom are far more intelligent than I, have now reduced me to a state of confusion – it is a difficult enough chore simply to tell a story, without plaguing yourself with the question of why you are telling it. I wonder if this is the Achilles heel of intelligence – that it breeds more questions, many of them unanswerable, than it solves.

Why am I writing this history?

I am 36 years old, and though most of the principals of this story are still alive, three have passed away, most recently, and perhaps notably, Ahab. If I do not sacrifice myself to this story the deaths shall mount, and time will bury it beneath its cold and weighty indifference. I do not wish that to happen, for Tycho's story is an important one. At least it is important to me. I believe that Tycho needs to be remembered, and being his close friend the two years he lived in Gora I feel that affixing him in the world's memory is my duty.

Besides, on long winter nights, with a heart too old and joints too sore for reveling, I have little else to do.

2

PAWEL OF GORA

At the age of thirteen, when I kissed my mother goodbye and set off into the greater world, I would never have believed that my journey would end with Pawel in Gora. Like most boys I half believed that Pawel was a myth, for surely the deeds accredited to him could not be true.

But they were.

In 1388 King Lukasz of Gora died. Gora was a tiny Kingdom near Prussia, populated by a smattering of Christians, but mostly by the pagans that the Teutonic Knights had been given Holy Orders to eradicate. Gora was so tiny that the Pope, the Holy Roman Emperor, and most Christian Kings, save those in the eastern German lands, were unaware of its existence. The death of Lukasz was therefore of little importance.

Lukasz died without an heir, and three years of war began as different parties battled for the right of succession. When the wars ended, the victor was a 23 year old, bald headed warrior named Pawel – later known as Pawel the Shining, Pawel the Scholar, and then, simply, Pawel of Gora.

The young King strode through his newly won capital – a ragtag collection of muddy streets, starving peasants and rickety buildings. He stopped before his castle and stared at it disbelievingly, finally lifting a rock towards the castle to see if it would tumble into ruin as it seemed to threaten. The rock sent a gargoyle crashing to the ground but the rest of the castle remained standing. Pawel strode closer and spat on it.

An ambitious man, Pawel desired a Kingdom of which he could be proud, and that disgusted spit on the castle wall was the first act of what proved to be twenty years of war, as Pawel fought, and routed, Teutonic Knights, Lithuanians, a miscellany of Germans, sometime allies the Poles and Czechs, Pomeranians, and anyone else who possessed land that he desired.

Pawel came to be known as the Shining during these years of war. He shaved his face and head every week, believing that hair was good for nothing but obscuring your vision, collecting vermin, and giving an opponent something upon which to grasp. Too arrogant to wear a helmet, the sun reportedly glittered on Pawel's bald head when he fought, causing it to shine like a beacon – an omen his soldiers believed promised them victory. Though he was not an Alexander, Pawel succeeded because he much resembled Germanicus; he was a solid, careful, patient strategist who slept on the ground with his soldiers, ate at their fires, and was able to command their allegiance even when their bellies were empty and their pay was months in arrears.

The growth and expansion of Gora was one of the greatest feats of empire building in modern history. Pawel transformed an inconsequential patch of impoverished farms into a grand and powerful non-Christian state, lying with Poland in that delicate area between the Germans and Kievan

Russia, an area which was the buffer between two different worlds – the Holy Roman Empire in the west, and the feared and ill understood Golden Horde in the east. Gora also held the distinction of occupying the area which had traditionally been the Mongols' doorway to Christendom. Due to its geographic importance, the emergence of Gora as a mighty state aroused much interest among western leaders. Pawel, who would be a very powerful ally, became a man to woo.

But the King of Gora would not tolerate meddling. At a time when the entire western world was controlled by the Catholic Church, Gora was controlled only by Pawel. Sneering at western Kings as lackeys, Pawel denied the Church any special privileges in his Kingdom, refused to communicate with Rome for years at a time, and openly aided the Hussites in their war against the Pope and the Holy Roman Emperor.

Pawel allowed a perfunctory Bishop to be posted in Gora, building for him a small church, but after a year the Bishop became so demoralized by his impotence and the total apathy directed at him that he wrote Rome, saying he would prefer to be a penniless Franciscan than spend another year under Pawel's thumb. When that Bishop left, years passed without another being appointed. The Roman Church, the true governing force in every country in Christendom, was largely denied a voice in Gora. Pawel, independent, headstrong, suspicious, atheistic and immensely powerful, became the only truly autonomous ruler in the west.

In Gora, as across Christendom, friends gather by fires to sing ballads, tell stories, and share jests. A man may hear of dragons who breathe flame, swords handed out by women who live in lakes, and the existence, somewhere in the wilds of Christendom, of the cup with which Christ drank his last sip of wine. We dismiss most of these legends as simply the products of fanciful imaginations. We know that minor deeds are exaggerated, and that the man acclaimed as the destructor of an army may simply have killed a rival in a drunken swordfight. It was with this knowledge that I had once believed Pawel to be a myth, at least in part, for in this age, a man and his legend rarely have more than one similarity – the man's name.

Pawel of Gora was one of those strange few for whom the truth was more fantastic than the fiction.

Pawel the Shining had once marched, not sleeping, eating as he'd walked, for two weeks without pause.

Pawel had raised himself from a sickbed and run into the fray of battle with a fractured arm roped to his chest. Literally single handed, he slaughtered fifteen enemies, rejuvenating his ailing soldiers and turning the tide of a battle that had seemed to be tilting against him.

With one thousand tired, bleeding men at his back, Pawel had sent a messenger across a river to a force of eight or nine thousand. The messenger pronounced "The first of your men to enter this river will lose his legs, the next shall lose his life, and from that point on you will find this to be a river of blood, carrying your lives away." The opposing general had scoffed, ordered his men to commence crossing the fords of the river, and then found that Pawel was indeed a man of his word. With the loss of perhaps a hundred of his own men, Pawel butchered an entire army, throwing bodies into the river, the discolouration of which caused villagers downstream to believe that the day of judgement had come.

In the years after 1411, when Pawel largely retired from the field, foreign leaders sometimes dispatched emissaries to meet with the King. They gave different excuses, but the true reason was always the same – they wanted to see if the great warrior had grown soft, if Gora was vulnerable. Pawel demoralized these emissaries. He would loom menacingly above the quivering man before him, speak through gritted teeth, and glare down upon him with a look that seemed to say "I'm going to eat your entrails."

But his true weapon was his legend.

The emissaries, already shaken by Pawel's colossal physical presence, would remember all the tales – how the man towering above them had massacred without mercy Teutonic Knights, gypsies, Prussians, even Papal legions. They thought of how Pawel had turned a river red with blood, and of a battlefield where Pawel's army had dug an individual grave for each dead enemy soldier, a number in the thousands. They had then cut off each fallen soldier's head, and placed them on stakes upon the graves as a message to that army's escaped commander. As they marched away, Pawel's men had looked over their shoulders to see an ocean of floating heads looking forlorn and miserable on the field where they'd fought their final battle.

This was Pawel of Gora.

1435

When Ahab advised me to start this history at the beginning, I asked him which one, for there are several smaller stories, each with its own beginning, which I must relate in order to fully explain Tycho and the life he led in Gora. Of the beginnings from which I had to choose were my own, Pawel's, Tycho's, Agnieszka's, who was the cook Tycho fled Gora with, the Burgundian Knight Beauvais, and perhaps even Bishop Tonnelli's.

This confusion of beginnings was much responsible for the year I spent planning, in great frustration, how to tell this story. I do now have a plan, but telling it to Alexandra she narrowed her eyes and uttered a very distressing "hmmmm."

The beginning of Pawel's story runs from 1391, when he became King, until 1417, when Prince Krysztoff was born. Tycho's story does not begin until 1429 when he arrived in Gora. Alexandra wonders if it would not be wisest to tell all about her father and mother at the outset, to make their story serve as firm ground upon which to build Tycho's story.

This does indeed sound a wise idea, but after listening to Tycho tell stories for two years I do not believe that wisdom is one of the more vital parts of storytelling. Tycho used to hoard his secrets, revealing them only when necessary, and that is what I shall do. I shall draw out Pawel's story, conceal his great secret until its revelation shall be the most surprising, and I shall begin Tycho's story before Pawel's is finished.

Rereading these words I sound confident in my plan, but rather than confident I think I am simply stubborn, and unwilling to delay my writing with any further debate. If I am to be honest, I should openly admit that I have no idea how to tell this story. My life's training has been as a jester, and riddles and jokes are quite different beasts from stories. A riddle is a quick teasing of the mind, while a joke is a creation of characters who shall be slain in a moment's time by a concluding witticism.

A story is more akin to constructing a boat, then setting it to sail towards some desired shore. Yet I am not a carpenter nor a navigator. In telling this story I am standing upon a beach, staring across a choppy sea at a shore I vaguely desire to reach. I need a story to reach this shore, so from the sand about me I collect driftwood and frayed ropes, securing them together with memories of Tycho's stories and the requirements set upon me by the goal I wish to achieve, the shore I wish to reach, the sea I must cross.

If I were wise I would finish Pawel's story, but I'm not wise. I'm a dwarf huddled under a fur, writing by candlelight, my hands covered in ink as though it were the blood of a dragon I am attempting to slay. Soon, too soon for Alexandra's taste, I shall introduce Tycho.

3

THE PLAYERS

GORA

Gora is the name of a Kingdom, but also the name of the city where the King keeps his court. The city is divided into three sections, and is cradled in the bend of a long flowing river which stretches from the mountains in the south, all the way north to the Baltic Sea. The castle of Gora sits upon a slight hillock at the northern edge of the city, overlooking the river. The castle area is completely surrounded by a high defensive wall, on the other side of which is the Old, or the Inner, city of Gora. The inner city contains the market square and belltower, along with many pubs and inns and shops.

The Inner city is surrounded by a second defensive wall, called the Barbican. Beyond the Barbican lies the Outer city of Gora. This is the outlying section of the city, home to most of the 20,000 who live in Gora. While the Inner city is kept in delicate upkeep, the cobbled streets cleared daily in the winter, local laws demanding the restoration of any buildings falling into disrepair, the Outer city is less closely regulated, and therefore more open, more exciting, a place where lives are closely entwined and life in general is more enthusiastically enjoyed.

Pawel built his Kingdom for himself, for the glory of ruling a vast and powerful land. But even as King he considered himself a soldier, and he lived a very austere life. He was little interested in arts or fashions or any of the other fineries, and yet he turned the city of Gora into one of the most vibrant cities and foremost centers of culture in Christendom. He built the Kingdom for himself – he built the city for his family.

Even before he had found a wife, Pawel was thinking of his children. He wanted for them all the pleasures and offerings of life, and his solution was to bring all the world's pleasures and offerings to Gora. He became a rival to the Medici in Florence as a patron to great artists. He sponsored architects from across the continent to work in the city, resulting in squares where modern, columned structures, reminiscent of the Romans, gazed across at the devils and monsters depicted upon the friezes of soaring, buttressed Gothic buildings.

Upon learning of the fabulously strange creatures living in Ethiopia, Pawel had pens constructed and elephants and giraffes and lions and tigers transported all the way to Gora. For a short time the city was the proud location of one of the only bestiaries in Christendom. Then winter fell, and the most exotic of the animals died under the fiendishly cold temperatures.

Painters came from the Italian peninsula and from the Low Countries, educators from Prague and Cracow. Astronomers and physicians from cities across Christendom dreamed of travelling to Gora and winning a post at Pawel's court. Mapmakers and geographers were hired by the dozens, copying old maps and producing new ones. Significantly, in this age, the mapmakers at Gora were ordered to leave their imaginations out of their work – there were no depictions of fanciful creatures at the borders of the seas, the tribes of Gog and Magog were left unrecorded, and, when necessary, "Terra Incognita" was faithfully recorded as such.

One of the most famous buildings in Gora was the city library. The commission for its construction had gone to a Roman architect who was obsessed with the beautiful simplicity of the circle. As a boy he had strolled daily about Hadrian's Pantheon, marvelling at the glorious ingenuity of its construction, but also imagining a building where the Pantheon's marvelous dome was supported by a base similarly round. It was in Gora that he designed the building of his boyhood imaginings.

Gora's library is topped by a dome of stained glass, supported atop walls of inwardly sloping concrete. When you enter the building, everything lies before you – the dozens of wooden tables sitting in the middle of the room, the few rows of upright book shelves and the one long circle of a wall which seems, from the inside, to consist entirely of books, as they stretch up the walls to twice the height of a man before giving way to the bare concrete upon which rests the airy and spacious covering dome of glass.

The library was completed years before any scrolls or books were acquired with which to fill it. When Pawel finally married, the new Queen worked with Ahab to assemble one of the finest collections of books in the world. They hired scribes by the dozens to produce copies of the Greek and Roman classics. They procured copies of Marco Polo, the letter of Prester John, Mandeville's travels, Dante, Chaucer, Ptolemy's Geography and Almagest – every writing of interest known to western man.

Pawel the Shining had been a warrior. When he withdrew from the field and turned his energy to the city, he gained a new title – the Scholar. As a warrior he built a Kingdom. As a scholar he built a city – a bustling, cultured city, inhabited by people of talent and housing works of beauty from around the world.

TYCHO

Tycho came to this city of wonders in 1429. He was sixteen years old and had spent his childhood begging his way through Christendom. I don't know if begging made Tycho a storyteller, of if it merely sharpened an already latent talent, but his stories made Tycho a very effective beggar. He would drop on his knees, in his ragged clothes, before a couple on the street and tell them his stories of woe – he had been orphaned by the plague (true); while carrying his baby sister (false) here to Basel or Strasbourg, or whichever city he was in and she had died of exposure (false); he needed funds to continue his journey to Rome, where he hoped to be trained for the priesthood (Rome interested him not for the priesthood, but because he was tired of shivering at night in damnably cold German fields).

When he told his beggars tales his passionate eloquence attracted crowds, his purse filled with coins, and often arguments would arise amongst his listeners as to who would take him home that night for a hearty supper and a warm bed.

Tycho never reached Rome, or any land south of the Alps. A few days out of Zurich, walking at midnight through a thick forest echoing with the eerie howls of wolves, he was stopped by a small band of mounted bandits. They demanded his money but Tycho, with the calm face of a card player, motioned to his clothes and replied "My Lords, surely you jest." The bandits regarded the boy more closely and realized that indeed their command had been foolish. The irony of the situation being that Tycho had had quite a run in Zurich, and likely possessed more money in his carefully hidden purse than all of these men combined. He had even been given a beautiful suit of clothes by a kindly lady in Zurich. But the boy, only nine years old, was already an expert regarding the dangers lurking on the roads of Christendom, and had sold the outfit and again donned the filthy rags he'd worn before.

The men asked Tycho if he would like to ride with them, and naively thinking it would quicken his journey to Rome, he agreed. In the company of a black sheep son of a noble Burgundian family, a Petrarch-spouting disbarred lawyer from Avignon, and a Franciscan monk sick of living hand to mouth while the Papal court wallowed in gluttony and avarice, Tycho spent a year robbing unwary travelers, breaking into farms to milk cows and steal eggs, looting churches, and listening to some of the most philosophical discussions ever held by three drunk and vagrant chicken thieves.

The road they followed, led, chaotically, to Prague, and after meeting Zizka, Tycho finally understood all the references to "Old One Eye" which had been spoken around their campfires. Tycho didn't understand the politics of the people he was now surrounded by, and didn't understand the bickering between Hussites and Taborites, but he had grown fond of his companions, he liked Zizka, and it did seem a shameful deceit that Sigismund had played on Jan Huss. If not in deed, Tycho became a soldier in lifestyle. He lived in camps with his friends. He watched as they marched out to battle, and when the battles were over he stayed with the wounded, telling crazy and bawdy stories that had them laughing through their pain.

When he was twelve, the disease which had orphaned him again entered his life. Zizka, who had defied the combined swords of the Pope and the Holy Roman Emperor, succumbed to the blotches and weakness of Christendom's greatest curse, and died in Prague of the plague. Of Tycho's three traveling companions, only the Burgundian still lived, and sitting with Tycho by the river, looking across at Prague

Castle, he informed Tycho that he was returning home. "I find it hard to consider this my war anymore," he told his young friend. "Especially now that Zizka is dead. Philip seems to be doing well at home. Would you like to come? As long as the Duke doesn't cut my head off we'll be okay." Tycho shook his head. He wasn't eager for another journey across Christendom. A few days later they said goodbye, Tycho waving as horse and rider disappeared from view.

Tycho remained in Bohemia for two more years, living in the camps, telling stories to the wounded, running errands and messages for Procopius, Zizka's successor, and most enjoyably, learning to use his silver tongue to woo girls at the market. The wars tired him though. They never ended. Nothing was ever settled. No one really won, and no one really lost. Tycho decided that he had had enough. He said goodbye to his remaining friends, enjoyed for the last time the charms of his Bohemian girlfriends, and ran his fingers over the various volumes of the Bible which Procopius presented him with. "Learn these stories," the great man told him. "They're seldom as entertaining as yours, but they'll lead you to Christ."

And then the road again. Town gave way to town, season to season. He slept in trees with birds and in stables with horses. His stomach growled. Sometimes his purse rang against his chest, other times it was sadly silent. Finally he was caught picking a pocket in a city called Gora.

It was a fine summer morning, the sun beating down from a clear sky. I was walking through the city market with Ahab, who was approximately sixty years old at the time. He touched my shoulder and pointed through the press of shouting, haggling people towards an immensely fat man whose purse was dangling out of his pocket as he leaned into the stall of a fruit seller, testing tomatoes. Then Ahab pointed to a young boy, obviously poor, who had also noticed the fat man's purse, and was now rubbing his chin in consideration.

The boy, with a well practiced movement, strolled past the fat man, lifted his purse, and was steps away without the man noticing anything amiss. Ahab, a smile on his face, watched the boy start to stroll away and then, with a few long strides, placed himself in the boy's path. Ahab smiled but remained silent, and watching them I could tell that the boy, Tycho, was confused – was this tall, ancient man standing in the way by accident or intention?

The market square is massive, and it was swarming that day, people circulating in waves of motion and colour. At the beginning I was the only witness to the drama which was unfolding between the boy and the aged man – not even the fat tomato purchaser had realized he'd been robbed. Ahab and Tycho stared at each other for several long moments, and then Tycho, taking a chance, simply started to walk away. Ahab, his tone more amused than reproachful, said "My son, I suppose you have an explanation for your little trick there."

Tycho turned back to the astronomer, looked him in the eye for a few seconds, and then took a deep breath. He didn't even appear nervous. "My Lord," he breathed, "as God is my witness, what I'm about to relate is the honest and unhappy truth. That man (and Tycho pointed an accusing finger at the tomato man), that gross and gluttonous man fondling tomatoes, is my father, though the Dominicans would need to put him on the rack to make him admit it.

"Sixteen years ago, when I was nothing but a swelling in my mother's stomach, he abandoned her, his lawful and wedded wife, leaving her in the hour of her greatest need to fend for herself on a crippled and war-torn farm surrounded by wolves and villainy." Tycho's voice rose and swelled as he spoke, causing a crowd to form. As I watched, people

31

shouldered their way towards the circle of open space in which the boy stood. He was magnetic, and the greater the crowd, the more powerful became his voice.

"My mother survived despite the poverty this deserter left her in, and when I was born, and when she had once again grown strong through the kindness of neighbours, also outraged at what this brute had done to her, she began a quest, one which took us through the Low Countries, through all the lands of the Germans and French, and finally to Zurich, where after twelve years, with what would be her last breath, she was able to stand before her long vanished husband, put her hands on my shoulders, and shout, with all the anger bred over her dozen years of searching – LOOK HARD YOU DESPICABLE FIEND! THIS, YOU ABOMINABLE COWARD, IS THE CHILD YOU LEFT IN MY BELLY ALL THOSE YEARS AGO!

"And so my Lord," Tycho continued, his audience seeming ready to burst into applause, "I buried my mother in Zurich, a city she did not even know, and there she lies in an unmarked grave because I had no money for a stone. AND THIS MAN (the accusing finger again) THIS MAN, still the coward he was twelve years earlier, far from acknowledging me, RAN from me." Tycho shook his head and wiped a hand across his brow, as though to demonstrate the burden life had placed upon his shoulders. "My Lord it has been four years now. I am sixteen years old and the only life I have known is that of the road. I have chased this man across all of Christendom. I have staggered through war torn fields, through villages empty save for the stench of the plague. I have no money, no home, and the only family I have, my father, refused to recognize me. Surely my Lord, surely you can understand why I felt it would not be a sin to take this man's purse."

The end of Tycho's speech was greeted with an amazed silence. The crowd paused, drew a breath, and became a mob. The fat man was lifted into the air upon a frenzy of hands and carried towards the castle. Tycho was hugged and kissed and showered under a stream of coins, assured by all that the King would force his father to make reparations.

When the crowd abated, when Tycho escaped the clutches of a bevy of teenage girls who had begun to fight over him, Ahab put his hand around Tycho's shoulders. "My lad," he said, "that was quite impressive. Wholly dishonest and highly embarrassing for the poor man you robbed, but impressive never the less. I find it hard even to decide whether to have you hung, I'm so taken with your story."

I saw Tycho speechless only a few times during our friendship, and the first time was that sunny afternoon in the market. Ahab had called the boy's bluff, and it was evident in the expression on Tycho's face that this had never before happened. He started to speak, but found his lips dry, leading him for several moments to attempt to work some saliva into his mouth. "My Lord," he said quietly, "I can return the purse."

"Indeed you can, and shall, return the purse. It is more the story you told which interests me. Have you told it before, in similar situations?"

Tycho shook his head. "No, my Lord."

"From where did it come so suddenly?"

Tycho, with a look of puzzlement in his eyes, looked up at Ahab, who hung in the air above him. "My Lord, I have never known from where my stories come."

Ahab seemed, for several seconds, to meditate upon the boy before him. He quietly asked for Tycho's name, and when the boy answered, Ahab said "I am a member of the court here, and if you desire, I can bring you into the employ of the King."

Tycho stared up at Ahab, amazement shining in his face, but upon seeing the interest in the lad's eyes, Ahab's brows furrowed seriously. "Do not answer hastily Tycho, there are certain conditions about life here which you would have to consent to first. Indeed, I may be in error even to make you this offer."

The boy listened to the astronomer's warning, pondered it for a week, and then decided that to turn away, to leave the renowned court of Gora, after a lifetime spent begging on the roads of Christendom, would be an act of gross stupidity.

We had a new court storyteller.

The first year Tycho spent with us at Gora he was like a child running frenzied through a kitchen full of Christmas delicacies. The gossip which arose about him was voluminous. I often sat in the castle kitchen, a mug of beer in my hand, listening to what the women said about the boy. What amused me most, as I watched them roll their eyes when his name was again mentioned in a less than lustrous light, was that they adored Tycho. They pretended they didn't, not wishing to be teased, but I could see it in their eyes, in their rapt attention when the boy walked into a room, in their troubled breathing when he touched his hands to their shoulders or hair.

I don't know what drew them to him, but it was much more than his youth and good looks. He was playful and irreverent and the aura of foreign lands hung about him. Tycho could speak a dozen languages fluently, he could tell those magical stories, twinkle his eyes seemingly at will, and when they twinkled for you it felt like you were sharing something with him, a sort of blissful astonishment at being alive.

It was also in the way he moved. Tycho eased through a room like a breeze across a field. He was around you, you raised your face to allow the wind to sweep close, and then he was gone, around a table talking to someone else. He was here and there, here and gone, coming and going, a smile for you a smile for someone else, and from watching him in the kitchen, in the dining hall, amongst crowds, I think what made him so sought after was that people felt a need to be alone with him, to possess him unreservedly, if only for a few short moments.

I have spoken, in the years since he left, to many people about Tycho. I asked the women why they chased him, why they desired him, when he was unabashedly a scamp who was sleeping with every woman in the castle. I asked other of our friends why it felt such a privilege to be alone with him, and I think we all knew, unconsciously, that the road was not yet done with Tycho, and that he had only been given to us for a short time.

Ahab has spoken to me of a Greek historian named Herodotus, and of his fascination with a people named the Scythians, who lived around the Black Sea. Ahab thought that Tycho resembled these people, who did not live in cities, or settle farms, but rather followed their herds of cattle across endless prairies, riding on wagons, carrying their tents with them. The Greek word for this way of life was apori – to be a nomad, to be without a home, to be inaccessible to others.

I have been a child of the road. I lived that life for three years, and Ahab, with his delight in things ancient, things intellectual, did not grasp the fundamental difference between Tycho and the Scythians. To be a Scythian, I imagine, was to carry your life with you – your family, your belongings, your past, your history. But Tycho was a single boy, an orphan, alone upon a road.

The road forces you to decide if your destination is worth the hardship – and making this decision is the traveler's burden. But Tycho was more than a traveler. He was a wanderer who did not even have a destination. I think it was this sadness which many of us saw in the boy, beneath the charm and the winning smile. We saw the sadness of a soul which would forever be in transit, which would never know a home, and which would forever be apori.

AHAB

As I was the court jester, my role to provide entertainment for the Prince and Princess, Tycho was the court storyteller. He told the children stories each night before bedtime, stories which both I, and later the children's cook Agnieszka, listened to as well.

When I spoke to Ahab a year ago about writing Tycho's history, he gave me a bundle of scrolls that contained all the stories Tycho had told the children. I sat in Ahab's study, the scrolls in my hands, my eyes near to watering. "How?" I asked, for I had not been aware that he had even heard those stories.

For two years, as Princess Alexandra, Prince Krysztoff, Agnieszka and I had sat in the story room, furs about us, a fire blazing, giving our imaginations to Tycho as though canvases upon which to paint his worlds, Ahab had stood in the next room, his ear pressed to a hole in the stone wall which admitted Tycho's voice to him. The old man listened to the stories and then returned to his study, where he put upon paper the wonders he had heard.

Ahab knew from the very beginning. I don't know how, perhaps his life's study of the stars allowed him to see brilliance in humans as well. I must now explain what Ahab knew, but prior to this, I should explain who he was.

Ahab was the one person in Gora who had known Pawel before he became King. They were the same age, but they weren't, and never had been, friends. They were contemporaries who had grown up in the same place at the same time, but in two very different worlds. While the young Pawel had been raised in the field by soldiers, the young Ahab had grown up at court, hiding away with the few other scholars then in the city. With them, he learned to love the feel of parchment under his fingers as other children love to feel their feet pound the ground as they run towards some distant horizon.

Ahab's father had been a member of the court of Pawel's predecessor, King Lukasz, but Ahab had never understood what his father's position had been – some sort of shadowy advisor whose council was considered invaluable by King Lukasz. In any case, Ahab rarely saw his father as they both travelled extensively, and by whatever quirk of chance, hardly ever together. His father was sent on frequent political missions and Ahab spent most of his teenage years studying at universities in Florence, Cologne, Prague and Krakow, learning Latin and Greek, philosophy, discourse, law. He learned as well how remote and backwards Gora was – how inconsequential it was, at that time, in the eyes of the world.

The death of his father occurred shortly before the death of Lukasz, but Ahab being in Florence at the time, a city that was barely cognizant of Gora's existence, he did not hear the many rumours which rose due to this suspicious coincidence. He stayed in Florence and then Rome through all the wars of succession and then, when Pawel took power, Ahab wrote the new King a respectful letter stating his intention to come home.

He returned to Gora when he was 23, and lived here without interruption until his death last year in 1434. He was the children's educator and infrequently an advisor to the King, but generally he was left to his own studies, and Ahab's passion, his quest, was to discern the movement of the stars.

If I were to paint a single picture to symbolize Ahab's life, the romantic one would be of the man standing in one of the turrets of the castle, his back straight, his face tilted towards a black quilt of a billion silvery pinpricks. But that image would be misleading. A truer image would be of an old man seated at a huge wooden table – a table littered with papers and manuscripts, knives and quills and candles, scraps of forgotten food and long overturned mugs. The old man is pressing a paper flat on the table with his left hand, while with his right he scribbles furiously, trying to keep pace with the frantic speed of his mind.

Ahab was a man devoted to learning, to his belief that the unknown could become known. When Tycho arrived in 1429 I had known Ahab for fourteen years. We were not friends as others would use that word – spending so much of himself in the realm of thought and theory, Ahab did not truly have friends, but we had grown used to each other. Knowing the old man as well as I did, I noticed how he changed when Tycho entered our lives.

Ahab's interest in the terrestrial world was limited almost solely to the Prince and Princess and his afternoon lessons with them. The rest of his time was spent in his observatory, his study, lost in thought. When Tycho arrived this began to change. Ahab took an interest in Tycho, gave to him some of the attention he'd long devoted to the stars, and became something of a mentor to the boy.

Seeing the Bible which Procopius had given Tycho, Ahab took it upon himself to teach the boy Latin. "It is a travesty," he said, "that you possess such a beautiful and valuable book, and are unable to truly appreciate what lies within." A few hours every day, for two years, the two of them were together, immersed in unraveling the secrets of the written word, and it was through this time together, and Ahab's secretive eavesdropping on Tycho's bedtime stories, that he began to suspect that Tycho was some manner of prodigy, a boy of destiny.

Ahab came to this belief largely because the boy had so many talents. He was multilingual and able to learn new languages seemingly through a single conversation with a foreigner. At sixteen years of age he had already travelled the length and breadth of Christendom. He had maps upon maps stored in his brain. He would meet a visitor to Gora, learn where the man was from, and say something akin to "Does that terrible old crone still have her inn near the bend of the river where that patch of birch trees stand?"

The boy was young and handsome, a natural born flirt and socialite, and when he spoke he drew people's imaginations and hearts with an ease that neither Ahab or I could believe. But most important were his stories.

He did not craft them, sitting alone by the fire dreaming up plots. Nor did he noticeably collect stories, drinking with strangers and listening to their tales. Tycho simply opened his mouth and they came, freely and gracefully, drifting from his imagination to ours. He could tell the ballads and romances of most storytellers and minnesingers, but Tycho's talents leapt far beyond those of his rivals, for the boy often seemed to be tied to the pulse of the world, and it was this, more than anything else, that drew Ahab's interest.

Tycho told stories that he could not possibly have known, and stories that had never been known, although they seemed indisputably true. He told tales of the Greeks and Romans, tales that were Biblical or elucidated on the Bible, and tales that seemed prophetic. Ahab began to suspect that our young friend, innocently and unconsciously, provided glimpses of the future.

To all of this Tycho was ignorant. The stories came and left on their own accord, and having always had the gift, Tycho was unaware that it was something unique. He did not notice the deep looks Ahab sometimes gave him, did not realize that the old man eavesdropped on his stories and recorded them in a ledger which he felt, if released into the greater world, would cause severe consternation, change lives, topple Kingdoms.

For Tycho told stories which although strange and distant, plucked strongly at the mind – the young pregnant widow who escaped across the Mediterranean after the crucifixion of her husband. The world that lay west across frigid seas, the knowledge of which resided only with northern tribes descended from history's most violent seafaring marauders. The vulgar German who set in motion a religious war which divided the most advanced land on earth in two.

What Ahab knew, before I or even Tycho himself, was that fate had presided over the boy's birth. I suppose it was the stars which gave him this belief, and the stars they say are infallible. Yet over the course of the boy's first year in Gora, as Ahab was growing positive that the boy was destined for some mission, I found it an incredibly difficult thing to believe. Tycho was sixteen years old. Daily I watched as he draped himself over girls' shoulders, planted kisses upon their cheeks, doused several with water and tore off through the courtyard laughing as he was pursued. That this child, this philanderer, might change the world....

I did not argue with Ahab, yet I could not believe him.

1435

Last night, when I lay down my quill after finishing my writing, I did so with trembling fingers. I had settled Tycho upon the page. And Ahab as well. It seemed an audacious act – to presume to know my two friends so well as to record how they would go down in history. My god, it seems an act more in the province of a Greek or Roman hero, than a lowly dwarf from Cologne.

Alexandra has just returned the pages to me, and she has set my heart at ease. "Well done Samuel," she said, smiling beautifully. "Very well done, except…,"

The Princess objects to my portrayal of Tycho as a sex driven scamp. "Sam," she said, "I know that the castle gossips spoke of Tycho as having slept with every woman in Gora, but you must base your history upon truth rather than rumour, or it will be a very compromised book with which you are left."

I did not argue with Alexandra, she would merely have buried me under vocabulary I could not understand and logic I could not follow, but I'll not change my description of Tycho, for it is the truth, even if Alex wishes to deny it – until the winter of 1431, when Tycho began to settle with his soul, he entertained a woman in his room every night. I am not proud to admit this, for I know it was an act of base friendship, but I spent a good many of my sleepless nights in the hall outside Tycho's room, listening to the sounds of copulation issuing through the fur door, and so, in describing Tycho as a sexual enthusiast, I speak with authority.

I am in Tycho's old room now. I work in his room, which has lain empty since he left Gora four years ago. I wonder now, as I work here, often needing to drop my quill and warm my fingers by the flame of my candle, if the reason Tycho was so loathe to spend his nights alone was as much for survival as pleasure. Tycho's old room is easily the least comfortable in the castle, and perhaps he needed the warmth of a lover's body to carry him through the harsh nights of the winter season.

Tycho chose his room when he first arrived in Gora. He fell into a drunken sleep one night in a misbegotten gap between stone walls in the oldest, and most oddly constructed, section of the castle. Waking in the morning he looked about him and decided that this hollow in the walls would serve him well enough as a room. He draped a huge fur from a wooden rod and hung it in the opening to the hall, calling what was hidden behind the fur a room.

It has one window, which, being winter, I now have shuttered to the cold. In the room sits a narrow bed heaped with furs, and this chair and wooden desk upon which I write. The room does not have a fireplace, and my friends tell me that I am mad to work here. I agree, yet something here inspires me as does no other place. I sit in this cold stone room and images of my friend rise about me. Upon the narrow bed lying silently in the corner, in the shadows, I see Tycho's tired face looking towards me on mornings, or afternoons, or even evenings, when I had to wake him for some purpose – to escape an enraged husband, escort him to a court function.

At this desk, where I now sit, I imagine the boy studying his Latin, reading his Bible, writing a segment of his journal. I look towards the entrance and remember him holding the fur to the side for me, allowing me to pass him and enter the hall, where I would turn to see him step after me, the fur swinging closed behind him. His face would beam as we walked along, youth poured out of him, and I felt less like an aged, worthless dwarf simply through the infectious joy of my companion.

My friends who tell me it is mad to write in Tycho's room would understand if I explained to them what I've written here, yet I doubt the words would come to me if I tried; it seems too private a matter to discuss. That is one advantage of this art of writing – one has the courage to write what you will, for it is easy to believe your words will never be known.

4

THE LOVE STORY

AGNIESZKA

It was a certain stew apparently, with local wine and freshly baked bread, which brought Agnieszka to Pawel's attention. A royal ambassador, while returning to Gora from Berlin, stopped once at the small inn owned by Agnieszka's parents. "A small man, well dressed, very dignified," Pawel's envoy told her months later, trying to jog her memory of this visitor who had later raved about her cooking to King Pawel. Agnieszka shook her head and the envoy looked around at the others, and then bent low and whispered in her ear "a little weasel who likely propositioned you, or even your younger brother." Agnieszka looked up at him in surprise, and he nodded seriously, but no, it had been too long ago, and she could not remember.

This ambassador, of dubious reputation, had so enjoyed Agnieszka's cooking that he had carried the memory of his meal with him to Gora, where he had gushed to the King about this marvelous girl in the provinces whose fingers had turned meat and garden vegetables into the delights of

Heaven. The King, eager to secure a cook of such talent for his children, sent an envoy with a small contingent of men to her village, named Kozle, which sat on the far side of the Kingdom.

Agnieszka, twenty years old, sat with her parents, her younger brother, and her fiancé, listening to the envoy present the King's offer –for a year of her time, longer if she desired - riches. The amount of gold mentioned caused Agnieszka's mother to faint, and her father to walk into the field outside and gasp profanities at the sky.

The offer was one Agnieszka could not let pass. She looked towards her fiancé, Michal, who she had known her entire life. Not only their hearts, but also their hopes and dreams, were entwined. There were already tears in his eyes – working in the capital at the King's court would mean a year apart, but even Michal knew she could not refuse this opportunity.

Three days later, after Agnes and Michal enjoyed a quickly arranged and hastily enacted wedding, the King's men sat mounted in wait for their guest. With her family and friends all waiting on the dusty road that ran through her village, Agnieszka found herself on the far side of that famous line – the line between those who are staying, and those who are leaving – she was, for the first time, leaving.

She hugged, she wept, she waved. She lifted her head from her lover's shoulder and stepped backwards out of his arms as ribbons drifted in the air, dresses swirled, and dust danced slowly in rays of morning sunshine.

Waving hands.

Farewell.

Goodbye.

The first few nights she did not sleep, and although each night as they made camp the King's men offered to erect a modest tent for her, she politely declined. It was mid June, the nights were warm, and she valued the stars above privacy. She lay awake listening to the snores of the guards, the crackling of the fires, the shifting of the horses, watching her family, her home, her village, but mainly her husband, appear and disappear in the constellations.

Mornings came with a voice calling her name. Agnieszka would sit up and rub her eyes. Men saddled horses, stamped out fires. The dew on the grass shone in the morning sunlight. "Today?" she would ask the envoy, taking breakfast with him.

"A few days yet."

Fields inched past, the sun hit its noon peak and fell, the hooves of the horses stamped the dirt roads, each village rose as an echo of the last and then faded away behind them. The longer they rode the more Agnieszka's mind turned from the past to the future. She continued to decline the tent, but closed her eyes to the stars, falling asleep to dreams, not of the castle and the royal court, her position as cook to the Prince and Princess of Gora, but of her homecoming.

She was already thinking past her year at the castle. She was already thinking about returning home.

TYCHO'S JOURNAL

JUNE 1430

I dreamed last night of women, and though this would seem a pleasant sort of dream, mine was not. It was confusing, even frightening. I think it involved Marta, who was sleeping beside me, and Agnieszka, who I have been trying desperately to have sleep beside me.

After my bedtime story to the children, Sam and I moved to the kitchen, where we persuaded Marta to tap open a keg for us. We drank well into the night, and when Sam wandered off, Marta sat down in my lap, put her arms around me, and kissed me deeply on the lips. "Shall we go to your famous room then Tycho?" she asked.

I reached around her and half placed, half dropped, my mug on the table. It wobbled and rolled and fell off the other side. I put my hands on Marta's hips, gazed into her wet parted mouth, and asked "What do you mean famous?"

She took my face in her hands and raised my gaze from her mouth to her eyes. "You'll fall asleep as soon as you hit the bed, won't you."

I shook my head. With difficulty I moved her off my lap and stood up. I put my arm about her shoulders and let her lead me out of the kitchen and into the stone hall. "I'll be fine Mary. Marta. Why did you say famous?'

"Oh you know," she replied. She held me close against her, her arm about my waist, her other hand securing my arm across her shoulders. "No, I don't," I said. She sighed as an answer. We moved on through the dark hall and when we started to climb the first staircase I tried again. "Tell me Marta."

She lifted me up the last few steps of the staircase and then stopped for a few minutes. A torch flamed on the wall on her right. Breathing heavily, she ran her fingers over my lips, swept through my hair. She kissed me, pressing her tongue into my mouth.

"Tell me Marta."

She pulled her face away, looked into my eyes, shook her head, and tugged me again down the hall towards my room. "Tycho," she said, gasping from the exertion of carting me about the castle, "don't play the half-wit. You know what I meant. It's just that all the girls have been here, haven't they? We all gossip about you, and have a good laugh about you. You're the castle scamp, and when new girls arrive at the castle one of the first things they are warned about is the storyteller Tycho's bedroom. That is why I said famous."

She swept the fur hanging in my doorway aside and we entered the narrow darkness of my small room. She dropped her arm from my waist and I moved slowly to my bed. I watched Marta take a few candles out into the hall, return with them alight, place them on the desk, and begin to unlace her blouse. Soon her dress dropped to her feet with the soft shush of rustling cloth.

When we finished, Marta nestled herself tight to me, massaged my belly with her fingers, and covered my chest and neck in soft kisses. She asked for a story. I felt adrift for some reason, and the story which rose to my lips was of a water nymph living in a great river. The nymph fell in love with a boy she saw bathing in the river, and so drew herself up into the form of a human female, walked slowly towards the amazed boy, wrapped her watery arms around his shoulders, touched her lips to his.

Hearing deep steady breaths, I lifted my head slightly to look at Marta's face. She was asleep. I let the story die. I didn't grace her sleeping ears with the tale of the love affair, the drought, and the man's long trek along a dry riverbed until finally he reached the sea and once again found himself in his lover's arms.

Instead I raised myself up on my elbow and watched Marta sleeping.

She is in her early twenties. We sleep together often. One of us seeks the other, we retire to my room, and in the morning we continue our separate lives.

I touched a finger softly against her lips. She didn't notice for several seconds, and then, slowly, she turned her face away until my finger was pressing lightly upon her cheek. I traced a long slow line from her cheek to her ear, down along her neck, under the blankets, through the valley between her breasts, and finally I lay my hand on the soft rise of her stomach.

I like Marta, but as she had said, many girls are in the habit of sleeping in my room, and I like them as well. I like them, but I don't need them, and to be fair, I don't imagine they need me.

I straightened my arm and lowered my head and upper body onto the bed. With my face turned towards Marta, I watched her breasts rise and fall with her breathing. Above her sleeping form, across the room and through the window, I could see stars.

The night drifted past and I lay quietly as Marta turned onto her side, facing me. I lay still as her sleepy hands touched and explored my body, as she pressed her head into the hollow of my neck, as my nose was swept by the scent of her hair. I felt that something was amiss, and when I finally fell asleep I dreamed of my bed, of lying alone in a tangle of blankets, and of a parade of faceless girls, each of whom stopped and turned and curtsied to me before disappearing out the door.

PAWEL AND KRISTINA

Pawel began actively searching for a wife when he was forty-four years old. The trouble was in finding a nation which he deigned worthy of uniting through marriage to Gora. He loathed most German Kings, and those he called the "Romish" – the city states and Kingdoms of the Italian peninsula. He admired the Hussites and the Poland created by Vladislav II. Pawel, and the Hussite leader Zizka, had both been with the Polish at Tannenberg in 1410 when the Polish had broken the Teutonic Knights. Yet neither the Poles nor the Czechs had a Princess available to marry him. Pawel entered into a correspondence with Margaret I, the Queen of Denmark, Norway and Sweden. Margaret found Pawel his bride, a girl from a noble Swedish family. Her name was Kristina, and she was nineteen years old.

The following is the story, famous in Gora, of their first meeting.

Pawel and Kristina met a month before their wedding. When they were introduced, Pawel felt an emotion that he had never experienced before – Pawel the Shining, the Warrior King, was intimidated. The King knew that his young bride was superior to him. She had everything which he desired in a wife – intelligence, patience, knowledge, gentleness, wit, warmth. She had these qualities plus a thousand more. She was beautiful and she was young – twenty-five years his junior at a time when Pawel was eating as little as possible because it was such a trial for him to digest food. On a bright clear summer day, with sunshine pouring out of the blue sky, and with four hundred people watching in the market square, Pawel took the Swedish girl's hand and led her aside, steps away from the dignitaries about them.

"Princess Kristina," he said, "I look at you and I see youth, beauty, grace, kindness. In your eyes I see a reflection of myself, and find that I am the opposite of all your virtues. You have come a long way, and I will be delighted a month from now to take your hand in marriage, but is it what you desire? Princess, I feel that I do not deserve you, and I would hate for you to marry me because your father and I forced you to as part of a political pact. It is your life Kristina, believe me when I tell you I'd rather hear you say no, than say yes against your will."

He had spoken in Polish, a second language for them both, although Pawel was nearly fluent. The nineteen year old girl listened carefully, translating his words in her mind, and when he finished speaking and looked at her, awaiting a reply, she ran through her translation again. It was unbelievable. He had offered her a choice, given her the power to say "no", a courtesy perhaps never before given to a young bride in a culture of political marriages.

She looked up at the giant of a man before her, and when she smiled she saw the tension ease from his eyes. "Tak," she said, the Polish word for yes sliding off her tongue, and it must have struck her as odd that this most important word of her life was being spoken in a language other than her native Swedish.

She said it again, "Tak," and on an impulse Pawel took the blond girl into his arms, his face bright, embracing her as a cheer rang out from the hundreds of guests and spectators in the square.

Pawel and Kristina married in 1412. She was a devout Christian and he an atheist. There was a twenty-five year difference in their ages. Pawel was one of the most famous men in the east. It was for none of these reasons however that their marriage was one of the most notable of the era.

Kings and Queens of Christendom rarely love each other. Thrown together through politics, almost never meeting prior to the wedding, being of different nationalities with contrasting languages and customs, love is nearly impossible. Kings generally continue relationships with lovers they had known before their wedding, and when the new Queen arrives to find herself excluded from her husband's bed, she begins to enjoy affairs of her own.

Such are royal marriages in the Holy Roman Empire. What grew between Pawel and Kristina therefore, from the moment of that first embrace, was something few had ever seen. Kristina had come to Gora hoping, but not expecting, to love her husband. When Pawel had given her the opportunity to refuse him, practically granting the Swedish girl her freedom, and then when they had spontaneously and excitedly embraced before all the hundreds of onlookers, she had allowed herself to become hopeful. The months that followed confirmed her hopes, and one morning, when she once again awoke to find Pawel awake beside her, staring softly at her, she said words that made the King close his eyes briefly, open them again full of tears, and then reach his arms about her, pulling his wife against him in a bearhug that grew stronger the longer it lasted.

She loved him.

Pawel rarely said those words, but it was only necessary to observe him to understand the depth of his love. He was not comfortable unless some part of him was in contact with Kristina. Seated at the dinner table they held hands, standing together his arm was about her shoulders, pulling her to his side. If he passed behind her while she was seated, he would bend and bury his face in her long golden hair.

They embraced each time they entered the other's presence. If somehow separated at an entertainment their eyes would search for each other, and circulating through the waves of people, they always returned to the other's side. More than any blade or blow he had ever suffered, what quivered Pawel to his soul was simply to hear his golden haired wife whisper his name.

Pawel the Shining, after all those years of war, of battles and decisions and hardships endured alone, had found the person who made him whole. Marrying in 1412, Kristina gave birth to Alexandra in 1414. The city grew, the Kingdom was at peace, the love of the King and Queen swept through the court and into the people of the country. Gora was a land of unrivalled happiness.

1435

I have mentioned how Tycho left his journal in my room the night he and Agnieszka fled Gora. It is a scroll, or rather two scrolls, rolled together and bound, originally, with a leather lace. A finger's breadth of space is all that separates each entry. These entries are not numerous, and though it would be possible to include them all in this history, I shall not do so. I shall include only those which illustrate a progression or change in the boy's heart or thoughts. The bawdier ones, gleefully describing his exploits, I shall keep for myself.

When Alexandra returned to me these recent pages, she asked if Tycho had ever mentioned, in 1430, his dream of faceless women. I said no, and this caused her to shake her head, ever so slightly. "Samuel," she whispered, "the journal is his true self."

Perhaps she is right. I believed, during Tycho's two years in Gora, that I knew my friend very well. Yet after reading his journal I realize I was wrong. The boy did not speak to me of the voices and ghosts which came to him in 1431, nor did he mention his conversations with Bishop Tonnelli or the Knight, Beauvais.

He kept much secret from us, from me. I am tempted to write that he held a mask before him, concealing, behind its smile, his true self, and yet I cannot wholly believe this, for it sounds deceitful, and deceit was not a part of Tycho's nature.

I did not know my friend; perhaps that is all I wish to say. I saw the shadows behind his smile and bouncing gait, but I did not know their nature until years after he was gone, when he was part of the past, and I had learned to read his written words.

5

1417

TYCHO AND AGNIESZKA

Gora was, and continues to be today, a prosperous city aswirl with activity. In summer months we were swarmed by travelling scholars, eager to copy texts from our library and to meet the famous Ahab. Emissaries arrived from foreign lands for diplomatic talks with Pawel, though often, if Pawel was not so inclined, they settled happily for Alexandra and Krysztoff. The poor came to beg the King for favours. Merchants enlisted lawyers who preened about court trying to win royal favour for their employers. Elaborate dinners were held, as were festive gatherings at which romances arose, causing gossip to bubble, and once, a duel to be fought.

To many, this was Gora - a city of high drama and plentiful entertainments. My Gora was much different, and more humble. It was centered about the story room, the well furnished and amply heated room in which Tycho entertained us with his imagination. We met nightly for two years - Princess Alexandra and Prince Krysztoff, me, Agnieszka for the second year, Tycho, and in his odd, owlish way, Ahab. We were a clique, the King's children and their favourites. We were our own circle, independent from and often oblivious to the greater goings on of the court. We were, and I think we all felt this way, a family.

Agnieszka made us a family. She became our older sister, the steady centre of our various lives. It was her warmth and quiet strength that sheltered us when loneliness or fear grew high, and it was her presence that made the rooms we met in feel like home. Tycho, an orphan who knew not even his nationality, came to depend greatly on Agnieszka. I was his best friend and she his moral guide, and it strikes me as quite amusing now, knowing the deep friendship they would come to share, when I remember the first few months of their acquaintance. Through the summer and into the fall of 1430, Tycho was head over heels in lust with Agnes. Agnieszka was twenty to the boy's seventeen. She was undeniably beautiful, but I think the reason she drove Tycho to such distraction, when he had an entire castle of women willing to share their favours with him, was that she constantly and unhesitatingly told him "No."

I doubt that Tycho had ever heard "No" before. It intrigued him. He could never determine what she meant by it. Nor could he find a way to circumnavigate this word, for Tycho was more a lucky child than he was a seducing rake. He had never chased women; they had always thrown themselves at him. He was at a loss therefore, after he'd introduced himself to Agnieszka and proposed they retire to his room, when she had burst out laughing.

Having long depended on his stories and his youthful good looks, the boy was forced to find new ways of gaining Agnieszka's affections, and so he gave her presents, helped with her cooking chores, pretended to be absolutely brilliant, and when that was unsuccessful, pretended to be sweetly simple. He developed a knack for tumbling down staircases and arriving shaken and bruised at her feet. But when he offered Agnes a sore elbow or scraped forearm to kiss, she would simply roll her eyes, sigh, and beg him to cease clumsily trying to seduce her. He didn't listen. He took to bathing regularly, thinking that perhaps cleanliness would impress her. He pestered Ahab for pleasant scents and Ahab, not too old to enjoy a practical joke, covered the boy's face and neck with a honey mixture, and sent him off to become a human fly catcher and the source of such hilarity for Agnieszka that she fell from her chair laughing as Tycho tried to charm her while scratching and swatting at the insects flocking around him.

He told her stories that had sent Hussite soldiers groaning through restless nights, their dreams full of women and kisses and illicit love.

He told her the opposite - tales of love between Knight and Lady meant to rouse feelings of romance within her, feelings which Tycho would reap in the absence of Agnes's husband. But nothing worked, and the closest the boy came to stirring feelings within Agnieszka came from a totally spontaneous action, the consequences of which he did not perceive until it was over.

Tycho and I were moving down a flight of stairs which empty into a long hall, at one end of which lies the castle courtyard. When we were halfway down, a bent servant appeared below us, a bucket of water in each of her hands. The old woman stopped at the bottom of the stairs, and cast a long forlorn look up towards us.

Tycho sailed past me, leaping down the remainder of the steps five or six at a time. He landed beside the woman, took the buckets from her hands, turned and flew up the stairs with them. Depositing them at the top he scampered back down, smiled to the elderly servant, who was scowling despite Tycho's kindness, said "Good day old mother," and then we turned off down the hall on our way to the courtyard.

We heard Tycho's name called out behind us. Agnieszka had seen the whole encounter and was now about to climb the staircase behind the servant. "That was very kind, Tycho," she called to us. The boy was taken aback. Standing beside him, I could almost discern the frantic turning of his thoughts as he struggled for a way to take advantage of the situation. Agnieszka only waited a few seconds, then disappeared from view up the steps, leaving Tycho staring at the bottom of the empty staircase.

I tapped the boy on the elbow, accidentally hitting one of his recent bruises. "You must know that you're never going to sleep with her."

He gingerly rubbed his hand against his elbow. "If I never have her, at least the chase was amusing."

"You're covered in bruises and insect bites."

A smile broke across his face, and he turned to me. "Aye," he laughed, putting a hand on my shoulder, guiding me on into the courtyard.

Tycho never slept with Agnieszka, but not through a lack of effort. To all his many entreaties she shook her head, regarding him with a mixture of pity and annoyance, as though the boy were a simpleton unable to comprehend the meaning of "no."

I adored Agnieszka for refusing Tycho, and their encounters always left me chuckling. Tycho would proposition her, she would sigh and mutter "give me strength" as she turned away, and Tycho would watch her leave with a perplexed look on his face. At his side I would be straining to suppress my laughter, and Tycho, looking down at me, would say "Hush, Samuel."

THE STORY ROOM

The story I shall record here, taken from the ledger Ahab made of all Tycho's stories, was told in early October, 1430.

It was raining heavily outside, and due to the chill we had a fire blazing in the room. The large bed, with its headboard against the wall opposite the fireplace, was occupied by Krysztoff and Alexandra. The Prince and Princess sat up with their backs against cushions, blankets and furs pulled warmly to their chests.

Agnieszka sat in a large wooden chair beside the bed, her legs curled beneath her, a thick fur draped about her shoulders. Tycho, who had earlier been pacing about the room, now stood solemnly at the open window, gazing at the raindrops hitting the sill, the swollen, grey clouds, the distant fields.

I tossed a last log of wood upon the fire, stepped across the room through the mess of wooden toys which lay upon the floor, and sat in my chair, on the opposite side of the bed from Agnieszka. Tycho moved from the window to stand at the foot of the bed. He looked at us four in turn, then spoke the words with which he always began his stories.

"Close your eyes."

In Bruges there lived a merchant who was both rich, and a good, kind, caring Christian. he had married at the age of 25, his wife beautiful and loving. They had two children, and now, twelve years into their marriage, with a son aged ten and a daughter aged five, the wife was pregnant again.

The merchant and his wife shared a love built upon a deep and loyal friendship. As well as being husband and wife they were also best friends, they revered their children, and the children, products of this wondrous union, revered their parents in return.

The family was well known in Bruges, one of the outstanding families who were active members of the church, well respected by their friends and neighbours, and the merchant himself, with a thriving business, was a just and Christian voice on the city council.

His world was perfect. His purse was full, but more importantly so was his soul, overflowing with the love of his family, and about to be enriched further by the impending birth of a third child.

On an afternoon in her eighth month, a wave of pain swept through the merchant's wife, and her breath and pulse erupted. In the bedroom, behind a closed door, the doctor and midwives worked with her for hours. The merchant paced the house wringing his hands. He bumped into his son and daughter who were as nervous as he. They looked to each other without speaking, their eyes wide, then flinched as another cry rang out from the bedroom.

The night ticked past unbearably. Each time the bedroom door opened, as someone stepped out to fetch water or towels or simply to rest, the merchant and his children raced to the door, simply to be told "Nothing yet."

Then, as dawn was breaking, the children asleep in chairs in the sitting room, there rose a long period of silence. The merchant felt the lack of sound to be more significant than any noise he had ever heard. He turned away from the window and stood at the bottom of the steps, staring up the flight of stairs at the closed door of the bedroom. The door opened and the doctor appeared. Seeing the merchant staring up at him expectantly he visibly shuddered, steadying himself by placing a hand on the bannister. "They're both dead," he said. "We're sending for the priest."

Crushed, the merchant sat at home, oblivious to the world. His business suffered, his friends spoke of his soul being broken, and as the weeks passed it seemed to be true. He simply sat in a chair in the sitting room, staring vacantly at the floor.

It was a cry of pain which awoke him from his stupor. One morning, still dazed from sleep, the merchant's son fell halfway down the stairs, and although he received several scrapes, he began to cry more from shock than from pain. The merchant leapt up and ran to his son, and rocking him in his arms, he made a fateful decision.

He was a Christian but also a man of the earth, and he believed, as many did, in black magic, hobgoblins, vampires, incubi, and other such superstitions. The decision the merchant made was to seek out a notorious witch, a woman who reportedly lived in the swampy bogs near the sea and whose filthy and infested hut had been visited by some of the richest men and most ambitious people in the land, including more than one future King.

The merchant had known of her as long as he could remember, heard of her as a legend, and now searching for her, he found her to be as elusive as the truth within a legend. He spent weeks on horseback. He enquired about her everywhere, stopping old hags who he somehow suspected should know where the witch lived. His old friends feared for his sanity and the children became accustomed to the feel of their house empty of their father.

Finally, on a typically dreary and rainy night in the bogs, he was taken on a raft through weeds and cattails to a spit of land where the window of a dull shack glowed with the light of a fire. In a cloak spattered with mud, his hair flattened and streaming with rain, the merchant knocked on the door, which opened with the impact of his fist. He stepped inside and found an old woman sitting in a chair, staring at him. "You struggled long to find me," she said.

The merchant barely heard her. "My wife has died, in childbirth. Instead of gaining a child I lost my life's companion. I never want to lose someone I love again. I want you to arrange this for me."

The woman stood, took his cloak and hung it over a chair by the fire. She motioned for him to sit down, knelt by him and pulled off his soaked and muddy boots. She put them by the fire and handed him a cloth. Then she pulled another chair over and sat down in front of him. She stared at him. "You must be extremely careful," she said. "For I do indeed have the power to give you what you want."

"I want what I want," the merchant answered. "I never want to lose someone I love again."

There was an exchange of money. The merchant moved against the wall far from the fire and the woman set to work. Water was brought to a boil in a large black pot, potions and bottles emptied into the water, strange incantations recited, and as the steam rose it changed colour, issuing around the room licking the merchant's face with a rainbow tongue before seeping out the window and door to escape into the night.

The merchant, having lost all sense of time at his wife's death, stood near to the wall for ages not aware of anything save a growing terror which tingled at his scalp as the room grew hotter and seemed to burst with a malicious energy. Finally he found himself on a raft again, the sky lightening with the coming dawn, insects biting him, warm clothes wrapped around him. He was taken to a dock where, to his surprise, he found his horse tethered nearby. The boatman drifted away without a word and the merchant mounted his horse and allowed it to take him home.

He found the city to be strangely quiet, as though the inhabitants had decided to be mimes for a day, opening their mouths as he passed but declining to use their voices. At home he *simply sat on his horse when it stopped at the front door. As the minutes passed the animal, attune to his master's strange mood of late, began bumping the merchant's head against the top of the doorframe, waking him and encouraging him to climb down from the horse's back.*

He opened the front door, found one of his servants sitting on the steps numb in fright, found another huddled in a corner crying, and mounting the steps to his children's bedrooms he found his son lying motionlessly in bed, his body turned to marble, his face sculpted by a master hand in the peaceful repose of sleep. The merchant rose, went to his daughter's room, and found her in a similar state - sculpted lying on her side, her hair falling gently, amazingly gently for hair of marble, over her shoulders and face.

Void of emotion, the merchant left his daughter's room and sat at the top of the staircase. Leaning forward, his elbows on his knees, a muddle of thoughts came to him which would dominate and torture his mind, to the exclusion of all else, for the rest of his life.

"Everyone I love has been turned into a statue," he said to himself. Then he remembered the witch's warning and his own reply.

"You must be extremely careful, for I do indeed have the power to give you what you want."

"I want what I want," he'd replied, and the memory of this fateful moment swept cold through his soul. "I never again want to lose someone I love."

Agnieszka, Tycho and I were uniformly silent when we left the story room that night. The halls stretched empty and dark before us, lit only occasionally by torches hanging on the walls. Above me, and beside me, I could hear the rain beating upon the castle. I was moved beyond speech, the images of Tycho's story resonating in my mind as I was certain they did in Agnieszka's. We walked through the castle, only the rain and our echoing footsteps breaking the silence. Finally, Agnes turned to Tycho and said, in a quietly shaken voice, "I'm beginning to understand why Ahab praises you so highly."

In a shadowy stone hall, Agnes and Tycho gazed at each other, while I gazed up at them. Tycho, at this very tender and intimate moment, made a leap of logic which only he, with his young fixed mind, was capable. He responded with "Agnieszka, why will you not sleep with me?"

She paused just long enough to ensure that he hung upon her words, then she parted her lips slightly, and softly answered "I love my husband."

She left us, Tycho and I staring down the dark hall at her disappearing form. The rain drummed upon the castle walls. Agnieszka's footsteps died faintly away. With Tycho's story sounding in my memory, and with Agnieszka's profession of love ringing in my ears, a wave of anger swept through me. For Agnieszka to be in Gora, separated from her husband...

I was unable to speak to her for days afterwards. I avoided her company, fearing that she would read and question the shame and guilt and sorrow in my eyes.

TYCHO'S JOURNAL

OCTOBER 1430

"You know it is love," she hushed, between the many and minute kisses she was laying upon my chest, "when with every spasm of pleasure you receive, you hope your partner is being pleasured as well." She tossed her head and a shower of long hair washed across the bold face of the full moon, visible through the window. I felt her hand upon me and her tongue make a quick circle around my nipple. "It is love," she said, her voice seeming that of a midnight spirit rather than the animal presence I felt upon me, "when the climax you are concerned with is not your own, but your partner's. That is love."

"Is this love?" I asked. I was not even certain I had voiced the question, but I must have, for she responded - a laugh.

A short but significant laugh from the shadows.

1417

Once upon a time there was a King who loved his wife, and life in their Kingdom was a fairy tale - the sun shone, the land was plentiful, the people adored their King, and day of bliss followed day of bliss without interruption.

The day the Queen died, a shadow entered the fairy tale.

Kristina died in childbirth, giving Pawel a second child, a son, at the cost of her own life. Holding her hand, staring at her closed eyes, Pawel heard the cries of his newborn baby echoing in an adjoining room, and then, despite the force with which he was gripping her hand, and the intensity of his desire for her to live, she sighed once and slipped away, the tension easing from her body as she settled deeply into the bed.

Servants raced about the castle, dumping basins of water so that her soul would not drown. Word leaked into the city and crowds gathered wonderingly in the streets. A boy raced up the steps of the belltower in the market square and set the bell tolling as it had not sounded since the wars had ended nine years earlier.

All this time, Pawel sat in Kristina's bed chamber, holding her lifeless hand in his. He was becoming lost in a dream which would haunt him the rest of his days, as would the bells of mourning.

He dreamt that he had lost his wife.

1435

Alexandra asked if I have finished with her parents. I said no, there is one thing more. She nodded but remained silent, fearful, I think, of what was to come. I am fearful as well - like a conjurer I must soon drape the castle in shadows, and it seems a task for Tycho, not for me.

The Princess's other comment upon this section of the history concerned Tycho's story, and this is an old issue, one which vexed Ahab immensely. Alexandra asked if I was positive that it had been raining the night Tycho told this story, and I am, for I remember well the rain drumming upon the castle walls as Agnieszka said to Tycho, in that darkened hall, "I love my husband." (and then, after Agnes left us, Tycho turning to me in exasperation and saying "but her husband is not here!")

Alexandra wonders if I invented the rainy night to suit the story, but I did not. The question then arises, did Tycho select the story to suit the rainy night.

I don't know.

Ahab believed Tycho to be a conduit through which stories were funneled by some higher power. He believed this because the scope of Tycho's stories exceeded even Ahab's age and great learning, yet Tycho was only sixteen and had never studied. It was therefore impossible, Ahab would argue, for the boy to know tales of the Romans and Greeks and early Church fathers - tales which were scribbled upon only a few scrolls and codices, locked in secluded libraries, and read by only a handful of scholars.

So Ahab believed that Tycho did not choose his stories, that they flowed from him like a stream he could not control. I disagreed, for when Tycho desired to impress himself upon a girl, he chose stories which would accomplish this, and when he had been in Bohemia he had deliberately told comic stories which caused soldiers to forget their hurts.

Alexandra, with her mention of the rain, wonders if Tycho was like a stringed instrument, sounding with music due to a passing breeze. She thinks it possible that his stories were determined by the conditions around him - the weather, the mood of his listeners.

Perhaps the reason we could not grasp the boy's connection to his stories was that they seemed almost apart from him. He did not know their origin, was often unsure if his stories were real or imaginary, and they seemed unable to affect him.

Early in his career at Gora, Tycho told us a story of love gone ill which left Alex, Krysz and I breathless. Alexandra opened her eyes to see a smile upon the storyteller's face which was totally incongruous with the story he had told. "Tycho," she asked, "when you speak a tale such as this, are you not moved?"

"By a story?"

"Of course by a story!"

Tycho paused, and looking into Alexandra's face he seemed to realize that she would not allow him to deflect the conversation with jest. He looked away from the Princess, and replied "Alexandra, my heart has said far too many goodbyes to be moved by a fantasy, a fiction of imaginary places and beings."

"Do you say that stories are impotent things? Or that your heart is impervious to emotion?"

Once again looking towards Alex, Tycho smiled, then rose to stand at the foot of the bed. "I feel perhaps I've spoken too much this night. Would I be slighting you, Princess, were I to leave now?"

"No Tycho. As you wish."

From my vantage, here in 1435, this night seems long, long ago. Tycho had been with us a few months only, and it was on this night, for the first time, that Alexandra and I realized Tycho's heart was not as gay and bright as he'd have liked us to believe.

6

GORA'S SHADOWS

THE PICNIC

In mid-October autumn receded, for a short time, into summer. The days were warm and bright, and word spread through the castle of a picnic. Originally planned to be a small affair, when we finally rode through the city, our party numbered close to a hundred. There were entertainers, including me and Tycho, cooks and other kitchen staff to prepare and serve the food, guests from foreign lands, favourites from court circles, two squads of soldiers riding before and behind us, and the King and his children.

Pawel led us to a lake, a few hours ride from the city, which was famous with the locals for its quiet waters and long, sandy, eastern shore. The lake sat on the edge of a great expanse of wheat fields. To the north and east, starting only forty or fifty yards from the water, wheat stretched out immeasurably. To the south and west rolled gentle grassy hills, covered only thinly by forest.

The horses were tethered, soldiers set at lookout points surrounding the area, a long firepit dug for cooking, and

Tycho, Agnieszka and I were working within an hour of our arrival. Agnes toiled at the firepit through the morning and early afternoon. During these hours spent waiting for the food to be prepared, peopled strolled about the shining lake, guards organized a wrestling competition and bet wildly as bodies were tossed about, and Tycho and I and the minstrels strolled amongst the guests, providing entertainment where it seemed needed.

Tycho and I performed the same duty at the castle, walking about the festive dining hall bringing light to people's faces with jests and stories. I like to prepare when I'm to work a court entertainment. If French will be present I devise jibes about the English. I examine my jester's costume to ensure that my ribbons and tassels are secure, my cards and scarves well hidden. I hide in my room and simply rest, summoning the energy to create my jester's persona, summoning gaiety, summoning courage.

But Tycho did nothing, and still he outshone us all.

I would wake him in the afternoon and inform him that we were to perform that evening. He would shrug, wander off in search of ale or women, return to bed with one or the other, drag himself out of bed when I returned for him on my way to the dining hall, step into the bright and gay room, and even with his hair a mess and his clothes rumpled pitifully from sleep, the boy glittered.

Tycho would rise from a table where he had set a group of Knights to weeping, move to a table of women who soon burst into laughter at some obscene tale, and then he'd spot a travelling Churchman and dazzle him with some tale of Christ or the disciples that had never before been known. He would bounce up to the Prince and Princess, set them to smiling, and then bounce away again. He would relent and speak briefly to some woman who'd been signaling him the entire evening. Soon I would glance across the crowded swirling room and see the woman bent forward in laughter, her hand on Tycho's chest or shoulder for support.

Then he was beside me, his arm around my shoulders, batting the bells on my hat with his hand, and then he was gone again.

Ahab thought Tycho a genius for the content of his stories, and while I agree that his stories were remarkable, what truly amazed me was the endless stream of entertainment the boy could provide, regardless of audience, language, setting, or mood. A river of words flowed through that boy's imagination, and by merely opening his mouth the words formed themselves into stories that perfectly suited the imaginations they would touch.

At the picnic, with the sun streaming down, the lake sparkling brilliantly, Tycho worked his magic, the minstrels and I did our steady best, Agnieszka and the other cooks prepared a feast of chicken, steak, bread, vegetables, and ale, and after dinner, when many of the guests dozed while digesting their food, Pawel released the entertainers from our duties, and gave us permission to drink.

Tycho and I were soon drunkenly asleep on the beach. I was dreaming pleasantly when a hand shook my shoulder, and with difficulty I came back to consciousness. A shadowy face was peering down at me, and with the bright sky above hindering my sight, it took me a few moments to recognize the face as Agnieszka's. She put her finger to her lips and shushed me, then walked a few paces across the sand to where I now saw Alexandra and Krysztoff standing above Tycho. I sat up and watched as they bent low, put their hands upon my sleeping friend, and began rolling him across the beach.

They did it very well and very quickly, rolling him perhaps fifteen yards through the sand until they reached the water's edge, and they continued to roll him deeper into the water before bounding away back to the safety of the shore.

Tycho took the joke with ease. He sat up in the water and ran his hands through his hair, wiping his bangs from his eyes. He smiled at Agnieszka and the Prince and Princess who were bent forward in laughter, howling his name, and then he stood, stretched his arms wide, and rivers of water streamed off him into the sunlit brilliance of the lake.

I don't know why the three of them did not anticipate trouble as he walked towards them. Perhaps they were laughing too vigorously. With a beatific smile on his face Tycho reached his hands towards Alexandra and Krysztoff and enacted a dual twirl-and-toss that sent them both into the water. Before the children had finished rolling, Agnes was off and running with Tycho behind her. She tore straight up the beach, holding her dress up to her knees, and Tycho, drunk and drenched, had difficulty keeping pace with her.

Agnieszka raced off the sand, through the grass and entered the wheat field.

It was here that she and Tycho became friends.

TYCHO'S JOURNAL

OCTOBER 1430

A feeling of change had been upon me since we arrived at the picnic site. As the others settled the camp, tethered horses, dug the firepit, I sat in the sand of the beach, staring at the lake, at the sunshine sparkling like diamonds upon the water - diamonds which rocked on the low waves, moving to me in quiet ebbs, before washing to rest as wave met land. It had been long since I'd seen anything so quietly beautiful, and I was struck for a moment to remember my life upon the roads of Christendom. I found, sitting by the lake, that memories of ease and beauty, of flowing rivers, rolling hills, came to me much more powerfully than those of hunger and fear. It is odd, for during that time my life was more often miserable than happy.

Chasing after Agnieszka along the beach, her dress billowing about her legs, her long brown hair dancing about her shoulders, I felt that time had frozen, or at least slowed, and I was delighted. I thought that if the afterlife is merely a moment, an image in pause, which echoes endlessly through the reaches of the universe, and if this moment upon the beach were the one chosen to represent me, then I would be content. The sun pouring down upon us, the sand under our feet, Agnieszka laughing ahead of me, the shining lake, myself in full flight - it would, I thought, be an image from my life that I'd be happy to float with into eternity.

Agnieszka turned from the lake, crossed the stretch of beach, her feet touched grass, and I followed her briefly across the field until she crashed into the high stalks of wheat. I lost her immediately. When I reached the wall of wheat and began stepping after her, I could hear her crashing ahead of me, I could see crushed stalks, discern the trail broken by her hurtling body, but soon the sounds and traces stopped. I paused, and found myself lost in time again - alone in a jungle of high wheat stalks, the wind causing them to whisper together above my head, brush lightly against my body.

After an age I reached forward, parted the wheat, took one step, and then another.

She was not so far away. I perceived a pair of feet, ran my eyes along her legs to her upper body, her neck and face, and saw her eyes, shining in mischief. She lay upon the ground, on her side, her head propped upon her right hand. If it had been another woman I'd have fallen immediately beside her, wrapped my arms about her. But it was Agnieszka, and I stood uncertain for several long moments. Finally I began to pace.

I walked circles upon widening circles about Agnieszka, breaking wheat down with my footsteps. When I had created a small clearing I sat down beside Agnes on a bed of wheat stalks. I lay down on my back and stared from our little hideaway up towards the blue sky. Under the rustling of the wind, and the distant voices of the picnic, if I listened closely, I could hear Agnieszka breathing. My eyes closed, I created a picture of her in my mind - the gentle rise and fall of her chest, the bend of her legs, the colour and texture of her dress and blouse, her head lying on her outstretched arm, the fall of her hair about her face, her hand sweeping a loose lock back behind her ear.

Then her voice.

"What are you thinking Tycho?"

Such a tender voice.

Sunshine warm like a scarf across my eyes.

You're beautiful.

Silence.

Tycho....

Silence.

We drifted, children on a boat, rocking on gentle waves of sunshine. I slept and woke, woke and slept, and finally opened my eyes to find Agnieszka sitting against me, her knees pulled to her chest, her chin on her crossed arms, the small of her back against my side. "We need return to the others."

The sun had placed a healthy glow upon her skin, and I lay upon my bed of wheat knowing, with a certainty I've never before felt, that I couldn't, I wouldn't, sleep with Agnieszka. I care deeply for her, but the idea of something physical between us seems brutal, a betrayal.

I wonder if this is love.

With the late afternoon sunshine pouring down upon us, I stood and offered Agnieszka my hand. Her fingertips touched my palm and she was beside me. I found her eyes on mine, and for a few moments we stood gazing at each other, then, by some unspoken but mutual consent, we looked away.

Agnieszka stepped into and through the forest of wheat. I followed, my hand in hers, dazzled by the fall of her long brown hair against her shoulders.

THE GHOST

In the months following Kristina's death I became an insomniac, and I spent over a decade's worth of nights wandering the castle halls. I know, due to those long years of sleeplessness, all the secret movements of the midnight world. I know the secret rendezvous points of fleeting lovers; I've heard all the quiet words of farewell. I know where the cats go at night, how close they'll allow one to approach before the shining eyes whirl away and a flight of silent paws leaves you alone in a dark and lonely hall. I know, more painfully than any sound I've heard, the steady drip of the water clocks, how they ebb time by so slowly it seems lifetimes have passed before their cups are full.

And so, due to my insomnia, I was one of the first to witness a phenomenon which would cause Pawel's name to be mentioned in dark stories, told by hushed voices, across the land.

On a winter evening, well after midnight, I was walking through one of the long, stone halls of the castle. I was covered in sweaters, with a fur wrapped about my shoulders. On the walls, in their iron fixtures, burnt widely spaced torches. In their glow the hall was lit by a dancing combination of light and shadows.

A night like any other, yet as I moved down that hall I began to feel fear.

I stopped and stood still, listening to the sound of my footsteps die away. I glanced over my shoulder to see nothing but the stone walls of the hall meeting in a distant haze of darkness. I turned, intending to step forward again, when a chill struck my spine and rushed forcefully through my body. It was as though a hand of ice had touched my lower back. I froze, and the hair of my body straightened and became so rigid that the sleeves of my shirts and sweaters were lifted from my arms, my wool hat nearly hovered above my head.

There was, beside me, a presence. As it passed I had a sensation of familiarity, as though a face I knew was smiling towards me. The presence drifted on, leaving me behind in its wake, and as my clothes settled on my body and my temperature rose to normal, I had an insight - the smiling eyes I had somehow seen had been Kristina's.

At nearly the same instant as this thought struck me, I began to hear footsteps sounding behind me in the hall. I turned to see a large, looming shadow approach. I stepped to the side of the hall and the shadow moved past without noticing me - it was Pawel, he appeared as though sleepwalking, and he disappeared down the dark hall in pursuit of Kristina.

I followed.

The King paced the castle for hours, and I was often forced to run to keep pace with his monstrous footsteps. We breezed through dark and silent rooms, ran up the spiral staircases of guard towers only to turn and walk down again; went briefly out into the courtyard to struggle through drifts of snow, and then, finally, I turned a corner to see Pawel crouched down, his back against the cold dark stones of the wall, a torch burning just above him, lighting the right side of his face, casting his features in an orange glow. He was silent and unmoving - a statue. I sat down to watch him, hiding myself in the shadows of the curve of the wall.

Despite his age, and the complaints his knees must have been making, Pawel did not stir - remaining in his crouch for hours. I could not see what he was watching, but I had the chill again, the caress of a northern wind across my body. The Queen was in that hall, and I believe that she and Pawel were staring at each other, unable to touch or speak perhaps, but not unable to communicate.

In the years after Kristina's death, people began to whisper that Pawel was descending into madness. They spoke of his midnight chases through the castle, how he spoke to himself in deserted halls, and collapsed into tears in empty rooms. They said that the day Kristina died, something within Pawel had died as well, and that despite the passage of time, he was never able to recover.

I believe that he didn't wish to recover.

When he lost his wife, Pawel did not lose his love for her. He survived her passing by building a world that he could continue to share with Kristina, a world that many were fearful of due to its inherent ghosts and shadows. But for Pawel it was a world where Kristina continued to lie in bed beside him, where she beckoned him to follow, where she asked him to believe, and where she whispered his name.

Of all the accomplishments of Pawel of Gora, a man who had created a city and a Kingdom, it was this creation of a world to house his love, erected upon a foundation of utter sorrow, that I most admire.

1435

A few days have passed since I finished the first part of this history, of which Alexandra tells me I should be very proud. I have read it twice, and though I am rather sinfully proud, I feel that there is more which needs be told.

When I came to Gora I was sixteen years old, the same age as Tycho. But while Tycho had known many women, and was soon to know a whole castle more, I had only known one, and I had paid for her, and she had only accepted me because she found Troyden's personality more loathsome than my shrunken body.

I have not known many other dwarves, but the few I met during my travels were largely bitter about their lot in life. They were quick to take offense at jests and slights, and eager to grapple with a bully, as though in gouging out his eye or giving a sound cuff to his tackle they were repaying God in part for his cruel joke upon them.

I have never felt this way. Rather I became resigned to my fate, resigned to the fact that the world was a thing not quite perfectly made - there would always be cracks in a glass when you held it to the light, whenever you had money you also found an unpatched hole in your purse, and the companionship of a woman, as well as love, were delights to be hidden in a locked chest, placed on a high cupboard, far out of the reach of clambering dwarves.

In Gora, in 1415, that changed.

Kristina, with an elegance and effortlessness that stuns me even now, eighteen years later, took my hand and became the most intimate friend I had ever known. She brought me to play cards with her in the gardens, with her maids, where I listened delightedly to the castle gossip. She strolled with me through the city, and the people of Gora witnessed the

Queen speaking to me as a bosom companion. I was not a dwarf, an outcast, with Kristina. I was her friend, and her friendship allowed me, for the first time, to live fully. I was a man who had only viewed the world through a small window in an underground cell, and then was released, able to finally witness how vast and blue was the sky.

When Kristina died, I lost the woman of the garden and the city walks, the woman who had allowed me to live beyond my shortened frame, and I felt as though my soul had been murdered, but there was, as well, another manner of loss.

When I came to Gora in 1415, I was searching for love as a blind man searches for a wall after rising from bed - arms extended, fingers trembling, taking tentative steps thinking that surely love must be near. I was not yet desperate for love, I was young, and, most importantly, I had the model of the King and Queen before me.

Pawel and Kristina's marriage gave me a faith in love that I thought could never be shaken. I watched the King shudder at his wife's touch and believed that a similar love would find me, would chase the cold years of loneliness from my soul.

Pawel and Kristina gave me hope that I would have love in my own life. And then Kristina died.

The castle, once lit by a warm and glowing passion, came to be wrapped in the embrace of an everlasting midnight, and in this castle, his reason corrupted, a King wandered through the darkened halls of his once beloved home, tatters of the past brushing like November leaves against his feet.

While Pawel lost his wife, I lost my hope. I felt that love had been discredited, and I collapsed as though deprived of breath, my heart feebly gasping in a hollow void from which it would never rise.

When Tycho came to Gora in 1429, he entered a castle that had been haunted for twelve years; haunted by the ghost of a Queen, the madness of a King, and by love itself.

He came to a castle within which love had died.

PART TWO

7

THE COUNTESS OF MARGURITTE

THE COUNTESS

Snow fell steadily though lightly from an overcast sky. It was our first taste of winter, a chill December morning, and I was high in a tower which overlooked the castle courtyard. I had watched the horses and carriages of our visitor from Burgundy journey through the city streets. The train reached the courtyard and was now at rest. Several long, still moments hung in the air - snow fell, banners fluttered in the chill December wind, horses huffed great steamy gusts of breath through their nostrils, soldiers, silent and gaunt, sat dutifully upon their mounts.

Finally, in the cluster of figures where stood the Royal Family, I saw movement. Alexandra took her father's arm and led him slightly forward. They moved through the dusting of fallen snow towards the most finely equipped of the carriages. The door opened at their approach. A woman, elegant in dress but whose beauty I was unable to discern from my great height, stepped from the carriage, bowed to Pawel and kissed his hand, then curtsied to the Prince and Princess.

The Countess of Marguritte had been a widow since the age of 28 and was 33 when she entered our lives in December 1430. The Count, her husband, had died in a drunken and pointless duel with a German from Brandenburg. The German was a terrible swordsman but a marvelous drinker. After leading the count to such a state of intoxication that he could only stand wavering upon his feet, muttering obscenities at the sky, the German ran him through as easily as one would a scarecrow. The Count slumped to his knees on the grassy moonlit lawn on which they'd fought and muttered the memorable dying words "How goddamned pathetic. Done in by a sodden German."

Marguritte is a small land under the protectorship of the Duke of Burgundy. Upon her husband's death, the Countess allied Marguritte more closely to Burgundy, and began acting as an ambassador and diplomat for Philip The Good. Her journey to Gora was in fact a mission for Philip. In 1430 Burgundy was caught in the middle of the war between the English and French. Duke Philip was allied to the English, and yet it was a delicate alliance. Aside from political concerns, Philip shared the opinion of the rest of the continent that the English were a band of ill bred, foul mouthed swine, and he was understandably anxious to lessen the import of his ties to the isle of the goddams.

Philip had two nephews, both famous Knights. The younger of the two, Beauvais, was as yet unwed, and Philip had begun toying with the idea of marrying him to Alexandra of Gora, thereby gaining Pawel as an ally. The Countess of Marguritte, well regarded by Philip as a cunning and potent diplomat, had been sent to Gora to sound out the King and his daughter on the subjects of marriage and an alliance with Burgundy. She was also to prepare the court for the arrival of Beauvais, who would journey to Gora early in the New Year.

On the day of the Countess's arrival, the castle was aswirl with activity. Walking through the halls I found myself ducking away from people on the run. In the kitchen, where I had hoped to drink a mug of hot water and chew in peace at a crust of bread, I stopped near the door and goggled at the scene before me. People were flying about drawing supplies from the various cellars, stoking fires, barking instructions, collecting dishes, all of this necessary for the many meals which had to be prepared, with the Countess's party now swelling our ranks.

I was standing with my mouth slightly open, amazed at the frantic pace of movement, when a hand touched my arm, and turning, I saw a vision which slowed the pulse of my blood and the beating of my heart. "Are you the dwarf?" the girl asked.

I nodded dumbly, and the whirlwind of bodies, the sunlight streaming through the windows, the chill of the winter air, vanished from my mind. The girl before me was perhaps sixteen, half my age. She had strawberry blond hair and wide blue eyes with which she could have convinced me to run through a stone wall.

"Are you Tycho's friend?" she asked, and slowly regaining my senses, I realized that one of the reasons I was so dumbfounded was that she spoke Flemish, which I had not heard in many years, and which I understand, though find a chore to speak.

"Oui," I said, resorting to French, which I assumed she knew.

She smiled so sweetly I thought my legs would give way beneath me. "Ah pardon," she replied, turning now to French. "I was sent to fetch the storyteller Tycho. My mistress desires an interview with him. I have been unable to find him, but was told that you were his close friend, and could deliver him for me to the Countess. Is that true?"

I nodded, and as I did she reached her hand towards me, a movement I copied. I felt a tumbling of coins drop into my hand. "Please hurry," she said. "The Countess is ever so impatient. There shall be more money if you deliver him quickly."

I knocked two people over while running to Tycho's room, my haste due not to the coins but rather the opportunity to again spy the strawberry-haired girl. When I burst through the thick fur in Tycho's entranceway I found him with his arm about one of Alexandra's maids, her head nestled against his shoulder. Too excited to be envious I shook the boy from bed. Within seconds he was chasing me through the halls, dressing as he walked, pulling his blouse down over his shoulders, tightening his belt about his waist. "Sam! Sam!" he shouted. "What does she want with me?"

I did not turn or slow my pace, but merely shouted "Hurry!" over my shoulder. We raced through the halls, making a broad sweep around the courtyard to the wing of the castle where the Countess had been quartered. When we reached her door I raised my hand and struck the knocker. Tycho stood panting beside me and looking up at him I leapt to swipe his bangs from his eyes.

The door was opened by the vision, the strawberry blond, and I started to speak but trailed off as I noticed that she was not listening to me, but rather staring raptly at Tycho, who was already introducing himself to her, in Flemish. I glanced from my friend to the girl then pushed past her into the room, shaking my head and muttering curses about the young bastard as I did.

In the far corner of the large room I found the Countess seated at a desk, writing. I stood behind her for a few moments, then cleared my throat softly. The Countess turned, and as distracted as I was by the strawberry blond, the Countess's beauty struck me dumb. I fear my jaw may even have dropped.

Although over thirty, the Countess's life had been one of luxury, and time's passing had given a maturity to her appearance without making her look aged. She had long blond hair which was drawn into a bun behind her head. She was tall and supple, and the low cut bodice of her black dress revealed the rise of her breasts. Her blue eyes held mine in a seductive gaze, and her lips sent me into a daydream of a summer garden with the Countess bent over me, placing searing kisses upon my chest.

The flow of my imagination was halted by the sound of her voice. "Are you the dwarf?" Too enraptured to be sarcastic, I simply nodded. "Is the storyteller here?" I nodded again, and still seated she said, "Bring him forward."

I scurried back to the door, brushed by the girl seized Tycho's arm and began pulling him across the room. Almost immediately he dug his heels into the carpet and brought me to a halt. "Sam!" he whispered.

Turning, I discovered the boy smiling apologetically at me. "Sam," he repeated, "I'm sorry."

I didn't grasp what the matter was until my eyes began to roam down his form. I closed my eyes and shook my head. "You," I said slowly, "are truly beyond belief."

He shrugged. He wasn't even embarrassed for himself, but had apologized because he knew how discomfited I was going to be, introducing him to a foreign dignitary, while he stood with a generous protuberance in the crotch of the loose fitting pants he'd grabbed in the haste of leaving his room.

"Can you not..." I began, trying to invent something he could do, but standing in the middle of that luxurious room, nothing would come to my poor mind. I made a tentative motion as though to push on it, but this made the boy jump back from me. "Heavenly Father," I muttered, eyes to the ceiling. "Of all the times to give the boy an..." It was at this moment that I felt hands touch my shoulders. I was eased aside.

The Countess had risen from her desk, swept silently across the room, and observed my exchange with Tycho. Now, having removed me from the scene, she circled the boy, nodding her head assessingly. Finally she stopped before him and stared unflinchingly at his erection, which, perhaps due to his youth, had still not settled. "Young man," she said, "you'll be pleased to know that in comparison to you, many a man in France and Burgundy enters battle very poorly equipped."

Tycho didn't reply and I rolled my eyes towards Heaven. The Countess looked to me and said "Thank you." She also glanced across the room at the strawberry blond, who had been waiting silently all this time. "Thank you, Isabella," she said. "That will be all."

Of Tycho's three companions, those he'd met south of Zurich and then travelled with a year, finally landing in Bohemia, only one had survived the Hussite wars - Albert Braudel, the man from Burgundy who had invited Tycho to return with him to Philip the Good's court in Brussels. Tycho had declined and they'd parted. The Countess was Albert's sister.

She desired Tycho's help. In Marguritte she had heard vague rumours about a "genius" storyteller in Gora. Although only a young boy, it was told that he could reduce crowds to tears, make men on their deathbeds shake with laughter, cause some women to fly to nunneries, and others to his room. The Countess immediately connected the "genius" of Gora to a character from her brother's stories of the life he'd led after leaving Burgundy.

Albert had spoken, deep affection in his eyes, of a young silver tongued rascal who he'd met in a dark forest. This boy, he told her, this lad named Tycho, could take any situation you gave him, any unlikely hero, and create a tale which would render you speechless, awestruck by the images playing about in your mind. Albert had said that the boy had a talent which defied description. The Countess decided that these two storytellers must be one and the same. She was correct, and after meeting Tycho, impressing him with the news that Albert was her brother, she asked of Tycho a favour.

"She requested advice of me on how to secure Alexandra's hand for Beauvais."

Tycho, Agnieszka and I were in an alehouse in the Inner City. It was the evening of the Countess's arrival, and the house was bursting with newly arrived Burgundians. At our little table in the midst of the mayhem Agnieszka gaped at Tycho. "Why would she ask you?"

"We have a common friend - Albert."

"Yes, but to ask for your advice in a matter of love, especially when the woman in question is as intelligent and mature as our Alexandra..." Agnieszka paused a few seconds, staring at Tycho, trying to find the words. "I'm sorry Tycho, but it's the grossest absurdity I've heard for years."

Tycho smiled indulgently at her, then turned to me. "Isn't she endearing when she's insulting me?"

"What did you tell her?"

Tycho raised his mug to his lips, then became distracted briefly by an altercation close to us which nearly became a brawl. "Well, as Agnes said, I told the Countess that Alexandra was astonishingly intelligent, that she would never marry one she did not love, and that she would never love someone whose heart and mind were not equal to hers."

Agnes beamed and reached a hand across the table, grasping Tycho's wrist and squeezing it firmly. "Tycho!" she exclaimed, "did you really?"

"I did indeed. Have I surprised you Agnes?"

"Truly. I'd not have thought you capable of such a mature answer."

Tycho smiled and rose, reaching down for my empty mug. "Have a touch of faith Agnes," he said.

Agnieszka lifted her glass and drank down the remnants of her ale. She handed the glass to Tycho. "Oh I've faith," she said, too quietly in the din of the alehouse. Tycho took her cup and leant towards her. "What?" he asked, raising his voice to be heard. Agnes smiled and waved to indicate that she'd said nothing of importance and Tycho moved away from our table, disappearing into the swirl of bodies.

THE STORY ROOM

A dark December evening, scant days after the Countess had arrived in Gora. The windows of the story room were shuttered, a fire blazed mightily on the far side of the room, causing shadows on the walls to dance with partners of orange glowing light. The Prince and Princess lay amongst the pillows and covers of the bed. Agnieszka and I huddled on chairs under furs.

Tycho, with a fur draped over his shoulders, stood shivering at the foot of the bed, a grey ghostly mist escaping his lips when he breathed. He gazed in turn at the four of us, then grinned. He removed his fur and waved it into the air, allowing it to settle upon the bed, over the already well covered bodies of the Prince and Princess.

"Tycho!!" Krysztoff protested, "you'll freeze!"

"I'll not freeze," Tycho replied, his eyes shining. He jumped upon the bed and within seconds had squeezed himself down under the furs between Krysztoff and Alexandra. "Heaven," the boy sighed, weaseling himself lower under the covers, causing Krysz and Alex to squirm and shift as well.

"Tycho," Krysztoff moaned, "your body is an icicle."

"Tycho when did you last bathe?"

"Hush, Princess. Close your eyes."

The teenaged Prince of Kasch had died in an outbreak of the plague. Kasch was a land of steadily declining fortune, and after the prince's death, all hope for the land's survival depended upon the King's ability to arrange a favourable marriage for his lone remaining child – the Princess Yvonne.

What the King did not know, what was, in fact, the most closely kept secret in the Kingdom, was that Yvonne had long enjoyed a love affair with a peasant named Janusz.

They were both seventeen and had met as children, when the young stable hand had held the Princess's mount steady as she had prepared to go riding.

As they knew it must, the day came when Yvonne's father arranged a marriage for his daughter. The union would make an ally of a neighbouring kingdom and bring peace to the land. Janusz and Yvonne debated their options and finally resolved to disclose the truth of their relationship to the King. They hoped he would grasp the depth of their love and realize, no matter what hardships it may entail, that they could never be parted.

Janusz was promptly murdered, his hands severed from his arms due to the King's fear that the boy's ghost would return to strangle him. Despite Yvonne's grief, the wedding plans continued unimpeded, and the night came when Yvonne lay in bed praying for death, for it was her last night as a single woman – she would be wed the next day.

Death visited Yvonne that night, but not as the reaper she had expected, rather as a lover. Drifting between dream and consciousness, Yvonne felt, or dreamt, a ghostly kiss as soft as a brush of summer wind. She opened her eyes to see only darkness, but the touch of wind continued, and she spent the night in its arms, receiving and returning ghostly kisses. As morning came, as the ethereal body upon her released its embrace, a sense other than touch finally gave proof to her nocturnal visitor. As streaks of grey entered the morning sky, she heard her name whispered and saw, for the briefest moment, a shimmering vision of Janusz waving goodbye.

She was married. Her husband, an immature boy with no experience of women, consummated the wedding night to the best of his ability. The next day they spoke nary a word to each other, and this remained true through the succeeding months. Yet a change was occurring – Yvonne began to feel the sickness of the morning, the nausea of pregnancy, and the optimists at court suggested that perhaps a child would bring love to their bitter marriage.

But the child growing within Yvonne was not her husband's, and upon the day of birth, with the midwives gathered about, her anguished screams echoing through the halls, Yvonne delivered to the world its most mysterious child. The baby's wails filled the room, but the child was invisible to all save Yvonne.

Janusz's revenge on the King, and the man who had taken his love, was to impregnate Yvonne with a child that on every other day was a ghost, visible only to his mother's eyes. He gave the King a grandson who would spend half his life in the world of men, and half his life in the shadowy world of the spirits of the dead.

"Tycho, I am trying to recall, have you ever told a story of love which ended well?"

"They all end well - a baby who is one day alive in his mother's world, and the next walks with his father in the realm of the dead - that's brilliant."

"Which ended happily I mean."

"A love story that ended happily?" Tycho looked at the Princess in mock puzzlement. "Are there such things?"

"Scores. Strange that you do not know any."

"Perhaps I do. Perhaps I simply find them uninteresting."

"Perhaps," Agnieszka said, entering the conversation, "you are simply unable to believe that they are true."

Tycho's stories were often succeeded by long conversations, and often, as on this night, the subject was Tycho and his stories. Alexandra enjoyed questioning the boy, arguing with him if she felt a character had acted falsely, if an ending had been unjust. I rarely joined these conversations, content and happy simply to sit warm with my friends, listen to the girls attack Tycho, and Tycho cheerfully defend himself.

Krysztoff was thirteen years old in 1430. His days were long, spent in training, learning the diverse skills he would need as King. Exhausted at the end of the day he invariably succumbed to sleep following Tycho's stories - his eyes closed, his breathing soft as the others joked and teased beside him. In physical appearance Krysztoff was his father's boy, already stout and broad shouldered, promising a future strength of arm. He possessed a thick crop of dark brown hair, as did Pawel before he began shaving his head. Krysz had an innate athletic ability. He learned fighting skills quickly and thoroughly, and those who knew Krysz only from a distance marveled at how similar he was to his father.

And yet those who knew him personally, including Pawel, realized that while Kristina had not given her son much in the way of appearance, she had contributed greatly in other areas. She had given him a patience that was quite different from Pawel's often bullish behavior. Krysz explored things while his father captured them. If father and son were to walk along a river and spy a frog, Krysz would watch to see what it would do, while his father would capture it and then control what it did.

Alexandra was often said to be the reincarnation of her mother. She was sixteen years old and radiant, with clear white skin, sky blue eyes, and long naturally curly blond hair. Her temperament was her mother's as well - she instilled trust and comfort in those about her, she was staggeringly intelligent and articulate, and she was adored not only by those at court, but also by the common people of city and country.

Pawel saw his wife in his daughter as well. Sometimes he looked at Alexandra and could only weep.

Despite her beauty, her position and her age, Alexandra was not married, and an unmarried sixteen year old Princess is extremely rare. The reasons for this situation were various

-a few of the matches had been simply ludicrous. Only months before the Countess of Marguritte arrived, the Widow of Toulouse had brought her son Raymond to meet the Princess. In the throne room, where they were introduced, Alexandra stood formally and elegantly between her father and brother, while Raymond, eight years old, squirmed upon his feet, seemingly attempting to forge his right knee into his left, tugging at his mother's arm and announcing repeatedly that he must desperately pee.

Pawel was another reason that Alexandra was unwed. He had been biased years previous concerning the nationality of his own wife, and he was biased again regarding husbands for his daughter. Several potential suitors had been advised not to travel to Gora and seek Alexandra's hand simply because they were Prussian or English or Romish.

Alexandra herself was yet another reason that she had not married. I watched for years at ceremonies and parties, as men of all ages had waited expectantly for their introduction to Alexandra of Gora. Yet after meeting her, without being able to say exactly why, these men always parted from Alex feeling disappointed, perhaps even dismissed.

As part of the legacy of her Scandinavian blood, Alexandra was slightly taller than most women, and of more solid a stature. She was kind and beautiful, intelligent and charming, and yet, in an age of Knights and chivalry, she exuded a personal strength which exceeded that of any of the men who came to Gora intending to win her. Men would bow and kiss her hand, hoping deep in their romantic souls to find a lady who needed to be saved, but instead they found a woman capable of saving them. If Alexandra were the heroine of a chivalric romance, she would have the dragon's head chopped off before the white Knight arrived, and when he did arrive, mouth open, gaping at her deed, she would notice his horse was limping and offer to shoe the beast for him.

Alexandra's strength was evident from childhood, and she remains today one of the strongest and most loyal people I've ever known. It makes me laugh, when I write this about the strength of her character, to remember how Tycho could cause her to shake her head, sigh in annoyance, with his stories of love gone ill, his refusal to surrender during arguments to her common sense. I remember especially a smile of his which enraged her. He possessed a smirk which seemed to say "Yes, I know that you are correct, that I am entirely wrong, but that does not mean I shall agree with you."

Alexandra would be midway through a splendid discourse on a perceived crack within one of his stories, and Tycho would smile this smile, and Alex's words would vanish away, reducing her to shouting his name in exasperation.

Lord I miss the boy.

THE COUNTESS IN THE LIBRARY

The Widow of Toulouse, who I have mentioned bringing her son Raymond to Gora a few months prior to the Countess's arrival, was incensed at the Countess's apparent ability to succeed where she had failed - to win, through Alexandra's hand, an alliance with Gora. Full of loathing, the Widow was able to avoid the Countess for the first few weeks following her arrival. Quite by accident however, while she was in the city library with Tycho, the Widow found herself confronted with her rival.

Tycho had been sleeping with the Widow, who was scarcely thirty and hardly less beautiful than the Countess, since the night she'd arrived in Gora. At some point, perhaps during what I imagine were infrequent lulls between sex and sleep, they had discovered a shared interest in Chretien de Troyes, Capellanus, and Guillaume de Lorris. The Widow, a distant descendant of Eleanor of Aquitaine, patron to these troubadours of love, was much enraptured by their ideas, while Tycho found them the source of great merriment.

Through the snow which coated the streets of Gora, Tycho and the Widow had walked to the library to examine and discuss the love outlined by these writers, of whom the two had such differing opinions. Seated in the middle of that immense building, sunlight pouring through the stained-glass portions of the ceiling, diligent scholars working quietly at the tables around them, Tycho saw the Widow stiffen as the Countess walked in with Krysztoff, who was grudgingly taking the woman on a brief tour of the city. Seeing Tycho brought a bright smile to Krysztoff's face, probably seeing the storyteller as a means to escape his laboured conversation with the Countess.

The prince guided his charge towards his friend's table. The Widow stood, endured the introduction provided by Krysztoff, and motioning towards a row of upright shelving stands marked "THEOLOGI" asked the Countess "Would you like to stroll for a moment?"

The Countess nodded, a wily smile playing about her lips. The two women swept gracefully through the library, their skirts brushing the chairs upon which students and scribes were pouring through books, some rubbing blank parchments with pumice stones and then chalking them to remove the animal fats and prevent the ink from running. The two women disappeared behind the high row of shelves, and the studious, reflective silence of the library was broken.

"Hadn't you be returning home?"

"Filthy Cow!"

"I've heard from my spies that your snotty nosed son wet himself when introduced to Alexandra, won't it be embarrassing for you when a Knight of Burgundy wins the Princess's heart?"

"A Knight of Burgundy, it nearly makes me wretch. You are lucky, are you not, that Gora is so indifferent to news of the outside world? Perhaps I should tell the King of your escapades in Burgundy?"

"Escapades?"

"Oh yes, your court in Burgundy is well known in Toulouse, throughout Christendom in fact. Is the story about the stable boy and the stallion true by the way? I can't imagine it myself, such an immense..."

"Hush you vile bitch!"

The conversation apparently continued in a like manner for quite some time. Tycho and Krysztoff, along with everyone else in the room, heard every word spoken due to the harmonics of the library, which cause every sound to circle the room like a softly ascending bird before fading away into the high reaches of the building. Those present, all male, were straining to keep their laughter silent in order for the argument to continue. Tears flowed from eyes, hands were clasped across mouths, backs were bent so that foreheads rested upon tables, shoulders everywhere shook with mirth. The final blow came when the Widow suggested they find a volume of Physiologus, the second century Greek who had collected the beasts into a zoological catalogue. "Perhaps," the Widow said, "the Greek included passages concerning the sexual proclivities of each animal. You may find a lover capable of replacing your horse."

The scholars could contain themselves no longer - gales of laughter burst through the room.

1435

I've finally made Alexandra laugh. It appears, preoccupied as she was with the imminent arrival of Beauvais, the possibility that she would be wed to such a renowned Knight, that she had never heard the story of the Countess and the Widow in the library. I find this difficult to believe, for it is such a good story, but at least I've made her laugh - the Princess is beautiful when shaking with laughter, her eyes water and she raises her hand to her chin, as though to prevent herself from laughing too hard.

I have written of Alexandra and the obstacles she faced in finding a husband, and in making an agreeable alliance. She remains unmarried today. There is no shortage of suitors, at every court function I see a different visitor to Gora, handsome and finely dressed, bending to kiss her hand. She receives them politely, but none catch her heart.

In December 1430, the Countess, preparing for the arrival of Beauvais, interviewed nearly everyone at court who might have some insight into the state of Alexandra's heart. At the close of my interview with the Countess, she asked why none of Alex's previous suitors had succeeded in winning her love.

I did not speak to her of the Princess's strength, or of Pawel's pride, the things I mentioned earlier. I gave a much different answer, one which surprised the Countess greatly, and which, though dire and bleak, I believed in my soul to be the truth. "Alexandra is unwed," I said softly, my thoughts of Pawel and his midnight wanderings, "because this is an accursed castle, a castle which knows of love only how to bring its ruin."

My words rendered the Countess speechless. I had believed, for over a decade, that love was dead, yet I had never spoken my thoughts so plainly before. I found myself shaken, and looking into her beautiful eyes, I knew that I had chilled the Countess as well.

8

BISHOP TONNELLI

THE BISHOP

The Teutonic Knights were the dominant power in the Holy Roman Empire's northeastern corner for most of the 1300's. They waged a relentless crusade against pagans, often joined by western Kings, who journeyed east to massacre the unbaptized in order to earn their indulgences - their pardons from the Pope, exonerating them, in exchange for this slaughtering of innocents, for all their earthly sins. Duke Albert of Austria, when he came to Prussia in 1377, called his crusade a "Tanze mit den Heiden", or Dance with the Heathen.

I write this to emphasize how, in Christendom, there are non-Christians. Gora is especially infamous for this - the only Christians in this land are those, like me, who have come here from abroad. Pawel a true native son, never had religious instruction. It was Kristina who pushed for a church to be built in Gora, and who asked Rome for a priest, which Rome bettered by sending a Bishop.

The first Bishop we had in Gora was a good man who expected to transform Pawel's Kingdom into a Christian paradise. When the opposite happened, when he was so ignored by both the court and the people as to be rendered impotent, he returned, humbly, to Rome.

Years passed, and then we were sent Bishop Tonnelli.

I saw him first as I knelt, with a handful of others, in a pew in the church. Late afternoon daylight, stained purple and red and yellow by the glass in the one window, shone towards the altar. A wooden sculpture of Jesus, the one religious artifact in the city, hung on the wall above the altar.

When our new Bishop entered from a corner anteroom, I was lost in Jesus's sorrowful eyes. So engrossed was I, and so quiet and unassuming was the Bishop that first day, that it wasn't until he coughed and began to speak that I noticed him.

It was the beginning of a torturous relationship.

He was a loathsome man, utterly despicable, and virtually the entire population of the city would support me in this view. He was grotesquely huge - tall but more importantly fat, so fat he seemed to be concealing sacks of vegetables under his cassock. When you looked at him you saw a man on the verge of bursting, a man who seemed to be constantly perspiring with the strain of preventing this imminent explosion from happening.

At dinner, his hair matted to his head, his clothes damp and his face contorted in a strange leer, he would sit alone at a table, patiently and steadfastly gnawing and chomping and slurping a seeming mountain of food. The table and chairs on either side of him would be sticky with saliva and littered with morsels of food which he'd burped from his mouth. His burps, and his farts as well, were thunderous eruptions which caused moments of silence as people noticed dust falling from the rafters and wondered if the roof would collapse.

Physically he was a jest of nature, a man whose presence wasn't endured but suffered. And then there was Tonnelli the orator.

Before he came to Gora, and his coming here was a punishment meted out by Pope Martin V, Tonnelli had been rising swiftly through the hierarchy at the Papal Court in Rome. In Gora he was a secretive, reclusive man, but occasionally we were offered a glimpse of the talent which had powered Tonnelli's rise to the heights of the church.

Although it was rare, the spirit did sometimes seem to enter Tonnelli. He would begin calmly, and then gradually begin to tremble and shake, and Tonnelli, whose bulk gave him a presence of Biblical proportions, would smash his fist upon the altar to punctuate his shouted assaults on the Devil. His face turned purple, he covered ten rows of pews with the sweat that leapt from his feverish brow. He reached into scripture and pulled forth truth and love as though they were ancient monsters resisting extraction from their underground lairs. He promised that God was watching, that Jesus would return, that sins, even those of the Catholic Church, were being recorded, and that judgment would someday come.

Tonnelli was banished to Gora by Martin V in 1425. He died in 1431, shortly after Tycho and Agnieszka fled the city. Upon his death, in the process of clearing his rooms, a sheaf of letters was found that I was able to secure. Exiled into a Godless land, Tonnelli had no one with whom to discuss theological matters, a subject upon which he had great intelligence. He also lacked a confessor, and to fill these needs he wrote letters to Martin V, the man who had exiled him. The letters ranged in date from 1426 to 1431, and in subject from theological subtleties to observations of life in Gora, including thoughts upon Tycho and Agnes, to sometimes explicit descriptions of sins he had committed in his former life.

Bishop Tonnelli's letters were a great boon to me when I was struggling to learn my Latin. They interested me immensely, fixing me to my desk for long hours of close study, as I strove to understand the thoughts of a man who had both appalled and educated me.

I have decided to incorporate some of the Bishop's letters into my history of Tycho. The reason being that he does play a role of importance in this story - a role I did not recognize in 1431 and which I barely comprehend today. Tonnelli's letters will provide a far clearer picture of this riddle of a man than I could hope to in my halting words.

And a few further notes before I allow Tonnelli to speak. Alexandra, I suspect, would ask me to explain to that scholar who retrieves this history from a secluded library, why Tonnelli's letters were never sent to Rome. Perhaps a few were, I know of only the letters I have, and it may be possible that Tonnelli wrote others which did reach Martin V, but I consider this unlikely. In Gora, during Pawel's reign, finding a courier destined for Rome-was well nigh impossible. I believe Tonnelli kept his letters simply because he could not find a means of sending them.

And a note about Martin V. He was elected Pope in 1417 at the Council of Constance. He was the first Pope to hold undisputed power after the great schism during which there were two, and then, for one year, three different Popes ruling at once. Martin V's name, before he became head of the Catholic Church, was Odo Colonna, and it would appear that Bishop Tonnelli had known Colonna for many years.

TONNELLI

JULY 1426

Colonna:

It has been nearly a year since you exiled me to this pagan land. As you know, I was, originally, livid about your hypocritical decree - livid because I'd not been banished for my sins, but rather due to your fear that the College of Cardinals would become suspicious of our friendship, that they would investigate your acquaintance with one as vile as I, exposing your own various sins in the process.

While I would be quite happy for your rich pompous family to choke on the ill-gotten land you are securing for them through the Holy Office, my anger of the past year has much been spent. I no longer, for example, desire to see you flayed by a rapacious devil, the Lord watching, applauding the demon in his work.

Though this may sound astonishing, I have come to enjoy my life in the rogue Pawel's Kingdom. I live humbly and alone, preaching to an always meager congregation. I am the only man of the cloth in Gora, and this indeed is why I write to you. In Rome, when we were young, rising through the ranks of the Church while plunging nightly into brothels, we were wont to confess to each other. We did it largely in jest, trying to shock the other with our sins, yet as we grew older and fell out of this practice, I discovered that confessing to you had, surprisingly, given me consolation.

Odo, though such a distance separates us, I would like to use you as my Father Confessor.

Forgive me Father, for I have sinned.

A year in a foreign land, a year away from the embrace of the Church. Will it shock you if I declare that the sin which, not disturbs me, but intrigues me the most, is the ebbing of my faith? Born in a Catholic country, gazing, as mere babes, at the horrible depictions of demons feasting upon sinners' souls, depictions carved on the churches in which we pray, faith is a thing which we are taught, like our letters, rather than something learned through personal study, personal reflection.

I once had this manner of faith - an ingrained belief that the Lord, the Church, Scripture, my Holy superiors, Jesus himself, were unquestionably just, truthful, and right. But faith is a frail thing, and though I have altered much since coming to Gora, I think my faith began to leave me long before, when we were young, when, as priests, we envied the Bishops their whores, when, as Bishops, we envied the Cardinals their orgies.

I no longer have faith, Odo. I believe, perhaps more strongly than ever, in the Lord, yet my faith in Jesus Christ's divinity has been shaken, and my faith in the Holy Catholic Church, in your Church, well...

Gora possesses a library the quality of which I'd never have imagined. I have had the opportunity here to study the teachings of Huss and Wycliffe, the Cathar perfecti - our enemies. As I have read the works of these men I've increasingly grown to understand and respect them. Once I would have seen the Devil's hand in this, thought it an offense worth scourging, but now I believe it is God's hand guiding me.

111

Colonna, if we disregard our own dogma and propaganda, and study only the facts, there is no question that Wycliffe and Huss were right - there is no Biblical basis for Papal authority, nothing ever written to justify the Church's political power, and, as proven by the forging of the Donation of Constantine, the betrayal, in which we both participated, of Huss at Constance, and the absolute atrocity of our Crusade against the people of Languedoc, the Church is nothing but a viperous coven of power-mad sinners, more intent on hoarding God's gifts than teaching his word.

I am a perfect example.

My sins are legion - rape, gluttony, avarice, homosexuality. Perhaps the worst of these is the rape. I have not stalked women, assaulted them and left. I seduced them with the word of the Lord, held it above their heads like an axe which would fall if they refused to perform what I told them was God's bidding. When I released them, and they stumbled home, violated, it was not some unknown stranger they had to blame, but God himself.

With the exception of a sickly albino who gives himself to me willingly, I have not tasted of the flesh since arriving in Gora. Pawel, who I've not met and who I am informed spends his nights with the ghost of his wife, has little enough patience with the Church as it is. Should I practice my old sins, should rumours surface, it is certain he would part my head from my neck without a moment's thought. It is ironic, that in a Godless land, I have become almost chaste. I have also begun to feel ashamed of my old sins, the ruin I enforced upon others. Yet beside this shame of myself has grown a loathing of the Church. As base as I may be, am I not a child of the Church? Am I not a snake born of its mother?

Colonna, if you were able, as I have been, to view the Church from without, would you feel as disgusted as do I? The golden goblets, soaring churches of stained glass, fantastic artwork – yet Christ preached in markets and on hilltops.

The secrecy surrounding the mysteries - why are there not vernacular Bibles? Why should the laity not comprehend the Latin phrases they mumble like puppets? If they were to read the Bible they would realize they do not need the Church - that is our fear, isn't it Odo? To survive we must teach the masses only enough to feel ignorant, not enough to be actually enlightened, for if they are enlightened there shall be born a revolution - the veil of sanctity which drapes the Church will be lifted to reveal it as the bloated drooling Devil it truly is: a Devil so far from the scripture upon which it bases its power that to return to scripture would cost thousands of God's greedy servants their ill gotten wealth.

Odo I'm raving. Sweat rains upon this parchment, corrupting my tracings of ink. I must retire shortly, but shall leave you with this thought, something which I think needs to be studied closely:

Given the deceit and lies upon which your Church is based, a Church whose true purpose is to spread ignorance so that the accumulation of wealth and power can continue, how can any priest remain pure? How could we have remained pure?

Huss was pure, so we deceived and burnt him. Wycliffe was pure, so we retrieved his corpse from its thirty-one year rest underground and attempted to halt the spread of his ideas by burning his already lifeless body. But his ideas are still alive, though his body has died twice. The lesson, presumably, is that even the Church is unable to destroy the truth.

Odo, I began this as a confession, but it has turned rather into a condemnation. I have sinned, but my Church is sin incarnate. Perhaps you should motion for an alteration in the wording of the confession: "Forgive us Father, for we have become sin."

Perhaps that would make a better prayer.

Gieuseppi Tonnelli
Gora

1435

When the news reached me, in 1425, of a Bishop coming to take up residence in Gora, I was ecstatic. There had not been a man of the cloth in the Kingdom since 1418, when the previous Bishop had left. After seven years in a Godless land, I thought to be readmitted to the Lord's love, and I felt my faith being rekindled, a faith which had given me much comfort when young, and which I'd sorely missed in the years after Kristina's death.

Tonnelli was not what I'd anticipated.

In my new Bishop, I had wanted a brilliant, articulate, passionate man - a man who could prove to me, in the absence of earthly love, that the Lord's arms were open, waiting to receive me. I wanted to be told that the next world would be beautiful, that misery would not be the only emotion I would ever know.

In his weekly sermons, which he often seemed reluctant to give, Tonnelli was largely silent about the afterlife. He was, in fact, unlike any religious speaker I'd ever known. He rarely quoted scripture, mentioned the Church and the Papacy only in jest - jokes muttered so quickly we never caught them, and he often seemed to be enticing us to doubt and question him, which we never did, for to question a Bishop, even a priest, was unheard of.

Despite all these oddities, Tonnelli could be, at times, heart rending and powerful. He spoke of Jesus as a friend, as a brother, and beautifully communicated Jesus's unbiased love for the poor and the deprived of the world. He begged us to live by the principles of love and charity and community which Christ had preached, and allow nothing to corrupt our understanding of these things.

And here his sermons would end, sometimes abruptly; the congregation pleading to hear more. I only understand now, through my reading of Tonnelli's letters, why his sermons ended so quickly - if he had continued, he would have descended into vitriolic rants about the wickedness of the Catholic church, the errors and inconsistencies of the Bible, and he was not yet ready, in public, to do this.

I am, in 1435, a stronger man than I was in 1425, and Tonnelli, in some ways, aided this. There has, however, been a price. I no longer know what it is that I believe, for Tonnelli's letters destroyed many of the things which I had been taught were infallible. The priesthood was ruined for me when I read of the young virgin in Languedoc who refused to allow a priest her body. Enraged, he accused her of heresy and had her burnt.

The Papacy was ruined through a quotation of Petrarch:

"(At the Papal Court in Avignon) there is no piety, no charity, no faith, no reverence, no fear of god, nothing Holy, nothing just, nothing sacred. All you have ever heard or read of perfidy, deceit, hardness of pride, shamelessness and unrestrained debauch - in short every example of impiety and evil the world has to show you are collected here. Here one loses all good things, first liberty, then successively repose, happiness, faith, hope and charity."

And then scripture itself: was Jesus the son of God or Joseph? For it is mentioned several times that Jesus was descended, through Joseph, from the House of David. What then am I to make of the immaculate conception? Which claim would the early Church fathers have me believe?

Above all this confusion float the ideals of love, charity, and brotherhood, in which I want to have faith. Yet only by casting aside the Catholic Church and its instruments are these ideals clearly visible.

That is the strange gift given me by Tonnelli - a man guilty of sins more damning that I care to believe.

9

NEW YEAR'S EVE

NEW YEAR'S EVE

In the early evening of New Year's Eve, when the sun has set and winter's darkness has settled upon the city, two boys are sent from the castle to the bell tower in the market square. They grasp the dangling ropes and set the bells chiming, their echo sounding out into the night, across the snow laden city, into the surrounding countryside.

The chiming of the bells on New Year's Eve is a call, to those fortunate enough to have been invited, to a lavish dinner in the castle dining hall. The bells cause doors across the city to open and the invited to step forth, slip in the snow, and begin their trudge to the castle.

Since 1417 I have waited in the snow and darkness of the market square for the New Year's bells to ring. I stare up at the clock face, floating dimly in the night, and at the stars beyond, listening to the chimes which, for me, do not represent an invitation to a feast, but rather serve as a bitter reminder of the most disastrous event for which these bells ever tolled - Kristina's death.

On December 31st, 1430, as I shuffled my feet cold in the snow, my arms wrapped about my body, the ghost of my being escaping my lips with each breath, I closed my eyes against the sound of the bells, the darkness and madness they represented, and I found my thoughts turning to Agnieszka, to the darkness and madness rising about her.

Then I moved away, for a festival of light and sound, food and bodies, was awaiting its clown.

The castle dining hall was full, two hundred guests clamoring about the tables, hurling their voices gaily into the rafters. Flags, banners, ribbons and stars hung from the ceiling, blazing fires roared in the several fireplaces, torches burnt upon the walls, and when the serving girls had filled each glass with wine, Pawel rose and moved towards the raised stage which commanded a clear view of the entire room.

Once upon a time Pawel's New Year's speeches had been long affairs. When Kristina was alive he stood before the room, light shining brilliantly off his bald head, and spoke to us like a friendly and convivial God, thanking us for being part of his life. In later years he shuffled onto the stage regretfully, and it was painful to witness. He looked broken, with arthritic hands no longer able to control the world he'd created. He mumbled welcome and good tidings and called for dinner to be served, and then returned to the royal table, sitting down between his son and daughter.

After dinner Alexandra took the stage in lieu of her father. As Pawel had years earlier, Alexandra shone before us - the sixteen year old Princess, tall with long wavy blond hair and the remarkable poise of her mother. Upon the stage she gave a short speech and then introduced Tycho. "My friends," she called out, her voice ringing strongly through

119

the immense room, "we do have entertainment for you." Her eyes focused on her storyteller. "Tycho?"

Tycho crossed through the center of the room, stepping around tables, grinning as people clapped him on the back. Stepping onto the stage he kissed Alexandra on the cheek, the Princess then returning to the royal table. Alone on the stage Tycho looked briefly stunned by the hundreds of eyes trained upon him. He waved a hand at us, a slight and impish smile on his face, and said "Hello Everyone."

And from smiling and drunk faces, two hundred voices answered "HI TYCHO!"

Tycho ran a hand through his sandy brown hair, a slightly embarrassed grin on his face. "I know this will sound odd," he began, "but I always begin stories in this fashion. Please," he said, "close your eyes."

I looked out across the room before following Tycho's instruction. Two hundred people, most of them drunk and boisterous, had unhesitatingly closed their eyes. It was strange, this power Tycho had with audiences. I looked to Ahab to see if the old man was assessing his student, but at his table the old man had already closed his eyes. I looked back towards Tycho to find him watching me, in that immense room only we two had open eyes. He grinned and made a closing motion with his fingers before his face, and I closed my eyes.

Tycho's voice drifted out across the room.

There is a village in northern Sweden which is so distant and isolated that most Swedes are unfamiliar with its name. It is a place of perpetual snow where summer comes like a kiss on a dancefloor and is gone in the winkling of an eye. The name of the town is Svengung, and it has an extremely strange winter tradition.

About an hour's sleigh ride north of Svengung sits the castle of a very wealthy and mysterious man. The mystery is the source of his wealth, for he is not a King, nor a merchant, and he lives in a building the walls of which are perpetually resisting an ocean of snow. The rich man, whose name is Nicholas, never has visitors, and he never travels to Svengung for supplies. "How," the people wonder, "does he survive?"

There are also two more mysteries. While Nicholas is a tall and sturdy man of impressive bulk, and his wife, on the few occasions that she has been seen, is also a person of large girth, all the others in that snow bound castle are dwarves without even the heftiness of our friend Samuel. These are thin almost unbelievable people who must put their back against a wall when they sneeze so that they won't be blown across the room. A whole castle of such people. How did they all come to be together?

The final curiosity is the unending racket. Regardless of time, weather or season, whenever a traveller ventures near Nicholas's castle, an unmistakable hammering and sawing of construction is heard. For years and years they have been building something in that castle, and yet the fruits of this labour are a mystery – nothing is ever shipped out of the castle, nor does the castle grow. These are the mysteries of Nicholas.

These mysteries will not be solved today, for I plan to tell you of the ceremony the people of Svengung and Nicholas play out together. The origin of the tradition has been lost, and perhaps that is just as well, as it leaves us room to use our imaginations.

Every year, a week prior to the 25th of December, a hunting party of fifteen men armed only with nets embarks from Svengung. The men ride dog sleighs north to Nicholas's castle, near which they camp for a day, taking great care to stay out of sight. The men bide their time, staying on careful lookout until they spot a group of the little people leave the castle. Dressed in white and almost burrowing through the snow, the men close in on the little people in an ever tightening circle. Finally, with a great deal of hooting, the men bounce to their feet, cast their nets, and reel in their prey, chasing after any that scatter. With great ceremony they then lead their captives to the dog sleighs and transport them back to Svengung.

The little people are housed in a special lodge in the middle of the village. They are brought food and drink and various Nordic delicacies and are the special guests at a three day long festival of drunkenness and debauchery. On the last day of the festival a representative is chosen from amongst the village's teenage girls. The chosen girl takes a count of the little people, makes note of their names, and is sent off to Nicholas's castle, where she recites for him a special message:

Dear Sir

It is my honour to come to you from Svengung and present you with this message. We hold fourteen of your people hostage in our village. Please journey to Svengung on the night of the 24th with the usual gifts to barter for the return of your friends.
Yours truly,
the people of Svengung

And so, on December 24th, in a red sleigh pulled by reindeer, with bells tingling and ribbons flying and carrying a great sack full of toys, foods, gifts and tools, Nicholas comes dashing into Svengung where the people, on one day of the year, put aside their suspicions about him and welcome him like a long lost father, throwing their hats into the air, shouting and cheering and dancing like fools while he talks seriously with the town council, listens patiently to the price quoted for the release of his friends, pays the ransom, begs once again for this barbaric tradition to come to a close, loads up his drunken friends in his sleigh, and rides off into the now dark night while the people of Svengung run like children into the main lodge to ogle the pile of gifts lying in a heap on the floor. Then begins an immense and vicious wrestling competition, the victors allowed to claim the first gifts.

That, my friends, in a small town surprisingly close to the north pole in the snow covered land of Sweden, is the ceremony of December 24th and 25th.

Please open your eyes.

Tycho's story, being neither funny nor moving, simply odd, was met with a deep lull. Drunk, and sensing that my young friend might feel embarrassed, I began moving between tables towards the stage. The slight clapping which had been weakly sounding for Tycho began to swell as the crowd noticed me, and when I did take the stage, tripping as I climbed the steps, the room echoed with a loud, anticipatory applause.

They expected me to perform of course. They all knew me as a jester with a quick wit and dexterous hands for juggling. But I had not taken the stage to perform, rather with the vague idea of helping Tycho, and I now found myself rocking unsteadily upon my feet, gazing out over a sea of heads, lacking even the vaguest idea what I would do, now that I had focused the attention of two hundred people upon myself.

I gazed at the torches blazing on the walls, the decorations hanging from the ceiling, and I met the eyes of my friends - Agnes and Tycho standing together against one wall, Alexandra and Krysztoff, Ahab. I removed my jester's hat, the tiny bells on my costume tinkling with the movement. "You're expecting," I said, in a loud and calm voice, "to be soon clutching your bellies with laughter, but I feel not suited to play a jester tonight. I wonder if you would all take a full cup of wine in your hand, for perhaps I shall simply make a toast."

The audience began to stir and bubble. Serving girls wove between tables carrying pitchers, filling cups. Agnieszka noticed that I was without a drink and made her way to the stage. She rose up the steps and handed me a goblet of wine, touched a hand to my shoulder, smiled reassuringly, then left me again alone before two hundred people, all watching me intently.

Perhaps, if it had been anyone save Agnieszka who had brought me the wine, I would have been able to find the comedian within me, been able to speak gaily to that assembled crowd. But along with wine, Agnes had brought me sorrow. I thought of her strength and kindness, her warm heart, her husband away in Kozle, and of the secret which would leave her shattered when the day came, as it must, that it be revealed to her.

I made three toasts that evening - one to old friends, another to the poor and lonely, and a third for Agnieszka. "My last toast," I said slowly, "is for those who are far from the ones they love. Let us hope that they are able to find peace this New Year, and that the peace they find is able to support them their entire lives." I raised my cup into the air. "To solitary hearts."

When December arrives, when the snows begin to settle upon the country, a squad of soldiers is assigned the task of clearing the field north of Gora. They dig until strands of frozen grass are visible through the icy crust of snow. The clearing which appears is maintained throughout December, and often comes to be surrounded by immense walls of snow, some winters higher than two men, were one man to balance upon the other's shoulders.

In the last week of December slabs of ice are carted into the field. On December 28th anyone who desires - artists, sculptors, butchers, or farmers, may visit the field, select a block of ice, and begin work upon an ice sculpture which must be completed by the 31st. The judging of the ice sculptures, by Pawel and the children, is the final event of New Year's Eve.

On December 31, 1430, after the evening dinner had finished and the guests had left the castle, my little family stood in the courtyard, our feet covered with snow, shivering in the cold. Alexandra was tying a blindfold across Agnieszka's eyes. Tycho and Krysztoff and I stamped our feet nearby, impatient to depart for the Ice Field. It was approaching midnight. The castle, the city even, was alive. People were hurrying back and forth through the darkness, doors opened and closed, lights flashed, voices called and echoed.

Alexandra, on tiptoe beside Agnieszka, tugged a final knot into the blindfold. "There," she said. "Comfortable?"

"I still do not understand why this is necessary."

"This is the first time you shall see the Ice Field. I want you to be dazzled, and this will be more easily accomplished if you see everything at once."

"There again is that mysterious everything."

Alexandra hooked an arm through Agnes's, motioned to her brother who took Agnieszka's other arm, and then looked to me and Tycho. "Shall we?"

We moved through the castle courtyard towards the main gate. The doors of the gate were open wide, allowing a steady stream of people to pass in and out. Many were laughing, their cheeks red, many had chins tucked low against their chests, scarves across their faces, hands buried in folds of clothing. As we moved off I glanced over my shoulder. From the shadows four guards had, casually, begun walking behind us.

You must imagine a full moon hanging above a sea of white snow. A long meandering road is cut into the snow, white walls reaching up high on either side. Above are the stars, and along the road are evenly placed fires, burning in large stone bowls, casting an orange brilliance about them.

This is how one walks from the city to the Ice Field.

Agnieszka and Alexandra whispered and giggled together. Krysztoff, his arm through Agnes's, nodded and bowed to the people we passed. Tycho skipped about nodding to everyone we saw. He bowed to women who passed us going in the opposite direction. He ran ahead and leapt upon girls from behind, shouting "Boo!" if he knew them, or saying "Hi, my name's Tycho," if he didn't. Then he would return and pinch Agnieszka's nose or steal my hat. When I wasn't listening to the girls or being pestered by Tycho I stared at the high walls of snow. I felt on a ship, watching in awe as two waves rose in preparation to engulf me.

The walls of shimmering snow began to recede. The road gradually widened until, like a river entering the sea, it emptied into a huge openness. We led Agnes into the middle of the field and then stopped, and after a few moments of silence, a time spent gaping at the ice sculptures, Agnes groaned "Alexandra please..."

Alex loosened the knot. The blindfold dropped from Agnes's eyes.

Under a black canopy, glittering with moon and stars, we were standing in an immense clearing surrounded by high walls of snow. The clearing shone with a silvery and almost ethereal light. Fires burnt everywhere, dancing orange against the white snow. Hundreds of people, wrapped well in warm clothes, walked about, talking and laughing, moving from one of the marvels to another.

Perhaps thirty sculptures had been completed. They were evenly spaced in the field, standing on pedestals, each ringed by three fires in a triangular formation which provided the light necessary for viewing. Agnes had never seen an artwork before coming to Gora, and here she was surrounded by figures carved from shining and dazzling ice - angels with haunted eyes and wings straining to return to Heaven, animals crafted so perfectly they could have been the original image from which Plato tells us living things were created, humans so lifelike, and yet so icily ethereal, that one shuddered at the thought of being in the presence of ghosts.

Agnieszka spun slowly in a circle, holding her breath as the fires and crowds and sculptures passed before her eyes. She looked at Tycho who met her gaze and smiled, and then at Alexandra, who asked "So, Agnes?"

Agnes parted her lips but said nothing. Alex took her arm and the two walked away.

Tycho, Krysztoff and I watched the girls disappear into the crowds. We looked to each other, shrugged, and I moved towards a sculpture of a dog curled in sleep at its master's feet. The small audience around the statue parted when Krysztoff followed me, but he took hands, smiled and said kind words, making people relax. Tycho stood at my side, and after a short while I noticed a large burly man place himself near Tycho. The man didn't look for an instant at the sculpture, but rather stared intently at Tycho, who looked up at him, grinning cheerfully, and said "Hi."

Not relaxing the grim set of his face, the man replied "Who are you?"

"I'm Tycho."

The man nodded, stepped past Tycho and bowed to Krysz. "Prince Krysztoff," he said, "I'm about to do something which I shouldn't, not in your presence, but which I hope you will understand, it being a matter of honour after all."

"What do you propose to do?"

The man moved his eyes from the Prince to Tycho, and in a blur of movement he straightened his back, raised his right arm and fist, stepped slightly forward with his left foot, and then his entire right side hurtled at Tycho, a devastating movement of weight which, although only the man's fist hit Tycho, was powerful enough to spin the boy around once before he fell backwards onto the ground.

Krysz and I stood still, too surprised to move. The people about us stared as well, and the man, after his brief display of power, just hung above Tycho, panting. "That's for my Wife!" he shouted, and then, after another few moments of silence, he stepped back, bowed to the Prince, and walked away.

When I recovered from my shock I dropped to my knees beside my friend, who was staring, with foggy eyes, up at the stars. I whispered his name, put my hands on his cheeks, which made him wince, and then finally he blinked, focused his eyes upon me, and with the slightest of smiles upon his lips, whispered "I wonder which was his wife."

When the wind blew, flakes of snow swirled about the field. Although it made the night colder it was unspeakably beautiful - the stars in the black sky, the distant encircling wall, the people, the sculptures, the blazing fires, all seen through a brushing of snowflakes. Pawel arrived onto this scene unannounced. He was accompanied by Ahab, Pitor, Gora's chief of engineers, and Pratt, the captain of the castle guards - these last two were comrades of Pawel's from as long ago as the wars of succession. On Pawel's heels was the Countess, and the Countess, an expectant delight rising within her, was waiting impatiently for midnight and the judging of the sculptures.

As part of her mission to prepare King Pawel's court for the arrival of Beauvais, the Countess of Marguritte had done much research upon Gora before even leaving Burgundy. She had learned of the ice sculpture competition held on New Year's Eve and thinking that he might prove of use to her, she had enlisted the foremost artisan at Philip The Good's court, an Italian named Bonadi, to accompany her to Pawel's Kingdom.

In Gora the Countess had attempted not only to soften Alexandra towards marriage, but also to soften Pawel towards an alliance with Burgundy. She found Pawel little impressed with her words, scoffing when she hinted that Burgundy would soon be the preeminent power in Christendom. Conscious of her lack of success with Pawel, the Countess paid Bonadi to create an ice sculpture which would serve as a goodwill gesture from Burgundy to Gora, and demonstrate Burgundy's knowledge of Gora's traditions and history.

She desired a sculpture of Kristina.

Bonadi erected a wooden screen in the Ice Field. While his competitors worked in the open, in the bright light of sunny winter days, Bonadi worked in utter secrecy behind his screen. The secrecy concerning the project, and the already mysterious aura which surrounded the Countess, led to much gossip concerning what the vile Italian could possibly be doing behind his screen. Some speculated it would be an icy tribute to sexuality which would cause even the warrior King to blush. The sculpture proved though to have quite a different effect on the King.

At midnight, with the stars and black sky above, the crowds of spectators murmuring softly in anticipation, shuffling their feet due to the cold, and with Alexandra and Krysztoff at his side, Pawel moved from one sculpture to the next, sometimes conferring with his children, dictating grades to a scribe who followed behind.

The children spoke cheerfully to the sculptors who stood humbly beside their creations. They responded with jokes to comments from the crowd, they raised their eyebrows in confusion, trying to compare one work of unimaginable beauty to another.

Then they came to Bonadi.

With the Royal Family watching, Bonadi and an assistant removed the light wooden screens which had concealed the sculpture. The wind rose and snowflakes scuttled past, flames from fires snapped in the night, four hundred people stood with their mouths slightly open, their misty breath rising above the orange glow of the Ice Field, rising into the greater darkness of the winter sky. For long moments we stood in an icy suspension of time.

Bonadi had simply aged Alexandra. He had taken the Princess's appearance, added six years of age, and unknowingly created a likeness of Kristina which couldn't have been more accurate if the late Queen had posed for him. What most people saw was a strikingly beautiful woman. What I saw, what Ahab, Pratt, Piotr and perhaps Alexandra saw, was the ghost of a beloved but long dead Queen.

The King himself must have seen a vision from his midnight underworld, the ghost who led him on his dark wanderings through madness. He dropped to his knees before the image of his late wife, and softly touched his hands to the sculpture's wooden pedestal. He remained thus for hours.

When they realized their father had been stricken senseless, Alexandra and Krysztoff began to organize the return of all the spectators to the city. With the shuffling and movement of this occurring about me, I remained still, staring at the King, gazing upon the strength of his love, a love which had imprisoned me, and Ahab, and Tycho, and most regrettably, Agnieszka.

In 1417, months after the death of Kristina, my partner Troyden expressed to Pawel a desire to leave Gora. In response Pawel offered him greater compensation, which Troyden declined. The King began then to threaten Troyden, but the idiot convinced himself that Pawel's threats were mere bluster, and one night walked calmly through the inner city, through the gate of the Barbican wall. He was collected in the outer city by a party of soldiers. They finished him and buried him in the forest beyond the river, first taking the trouble to sever the tall clown's head from his body. I woke the next morning to a blood soaked pillow, my recently deceased partner's eyes staring at me, aghast.

Pawel had prized his children's' happiness even before the death of Kristina. After her death his concern and protectiveness of them became macabre. Troyden was the first victim of what was to become a highly secretive policy - the entertainers, educators, cooks or friends of Alexandra and Krysztoff, anyone who was in some way beneficial to them, were not permitted to leave Gora. In Pawel's steadily darkening mind, for a favourite of the children's to leave was a betrayal of their happiness, and only death was a fitting punishment.

Ahab, Tycho, Agnieszka and I were prisoners in Gora, able to move through the inner city, but unable to pass through the gates in the Barbican wall into the outer city without an escort of guards. Our imprisonment had been sprung upon Ahab and me, not altogether unhappily, and before Tycho had accepted the post of storyteller, Ahab had warned him of the likelihood that he would be imprisoned in Gora. Yet Agnieszka had been wooed to the castle with the lie that she would be able to return to Kozle at the end of a year.

It was this fact which had saddened me while on stage in the dining hall - Agnieszka was forever parted from her husband, Gora's curse upon love was well alive.

In the Ice Field, Ahab, Agnieszka, the Prince and Princess, Tycho and I, stood together gazing upon Pawel. The crowd gradually thinned, and when the field was nearly empty, Ahab suggested we leave the children alone with their father. Agnes hugged Alexandra and Krysztoff and moved away with Ahab. I lingered on hesitantly, for Tycho had shown no inclination to leave.

One of the guards who had accompanied our party to the Ice Field stepped to me through the silent night. "Samuel" he whispered, "we must return you and Tycho to the castle." I nodded, looking at my friend as he stared at the King. "I'll leave," I answered. "But can not Tycho remain? Several guards shall need stay with the Prince and Princess anyway, won't they?"

And so I bargained for Tycho a longer glimpse of Pawel's love. Before I turned down the snow walled road which led to the city, I paused a long while, my guard at my side, looking at the expanse of the Ice Field. I saw a black sky full of silvery stars and a large shining moon. I saw a field surrounded by a long circular wall of snow. In this field fires burnt, flapping their arms in the wind. I saw beautiful sculptures of ice standing on wooden pedestals, some so far away I could have mistaken them for living things. I saw a sixteen year old Princess, her long blond hair flowing from her woolen hat, standing alongside her thirteen year old brother. They were watching their father, who was now shaking as he knelt before the sculpture of his late wife. Away from the children was a young boy, a boy who stood with his arms clutched across his chest, not moving despite the cold. Finally I saw guards watching the Prince and Princess and King out of concern for their safety, and watching Tycho to prevent his possible escape.

I turned and moved along the road cut through the ocean of snow. The guard trudging at my side was silent, and I was glad, for speech would have ruined the walk, betrayed the sad and beautiful drama which had occurred. My thoughts were of my King and his attachment to the past, of my friend Agnieszka who would one day need be told the truth, and of my young friend, the storyteller, who was witnessing what it meant to lose the one you loved more than yourself.

1435

Alexandra has always believed that this rule of her father's, which kept her friends imprisoned in Gora, was Pawel's worst act of cruelty. She can rationalize the severing of a thousand heads as an act of war, but to enslave innocent people, she believes, was an act of madness.

I don't know.

After Kristina's death, Pawel walked half in her world of shadows, and half in the world she'd departed. The world in which Kristina had died, the world of the living, gave him nothing but misery, and the reason he did not renounce it entirely, stepping fully into Kristina's underworld, was his concern for his children.

Pawel continued to govern the Kingdom, to maintain its strength and peace, because he desired his children to inherit a healthy and prosperous land. He knew that if he went wholly into darkness, with his children still young, the country would be besieged by foreign invaders, and perhaps even weakened by dissent from within. He clutched onto the remnants of his sanity for the sake of his children, and perhaps the policy which imprisoned Ahab, Tycho, Agnes and I can be explained as simply a facet of his love for his children, misguided though it may have been.

I never felt a slave in Gora. I did not wish to leave, nor did Tycho or Ahab. The problem of our slavery was of import only to Agnieszka, and she did not become aware of her imprisonment until nearly the end of her year in Gora.

As soon as we grasped the depth of Agnes's love for Michal, and the fact that, unlike Tycho and me, she would truly feel a slave in Gora, we should have told Agnes about her imprisonment. Yet none of us - Tycho, Alex and Krysz., who knew of their father's rule but were unable to sway him from it, nor I, were brave enough to confront Agnes with the truth - a truth which we felt would shatter her.

And so we remained silent, through that winter of 1431, as the truth hung ominously in the air above us. We remained silent in the story room when Agnes reminisced about her home, and we hoped that she would somehow be delivered, that Gora's darkness would release her from its hold.

10

BEAUVAIS

AHAB AND TYCHO

When I was inspired by Tycho's journal, near the end of 1431, to decode for myself the words and lines and thoughts the boy had inscribed on the scrolls he'd left in my room, I went to Ahab and requested that he teach me the mysteries of the written word. The lessons I had with Ahab were strained, difficult things, full of grammar and vocabulary which slipped from my mind leaving me grasping for words like a stammering dunce. Ahab often leant back to regard me with an amused bewilderment upon his face. I was a much poorer student than Alexandra and Krysztoff, and even they had paled beside Tycho.

Tycho's reading lessons, which I occasionally attended, unable to find other entertainment, were not truly lessons. The boy simply read his Bible aloud, stopping when something confused him, and asked Ahab to clarify the passage. The universe of the written word was something that he seemed to have to remember, rather than learn, and he remembered it with an ease and virtuosity that startled Ahab.

Sometime in the weeks following Pawel's collapse in the Ice Field, an event which had hushed the entire castle, I was witness to an intriguing conversation between my two friends. It was evening in Ahab's study. The long table occupying the center of the room was covered with papers, candles and quills. Tycho and Ahab sat directly across from each other, Tycho bending forward to read from one of the codices of his Bible, which lay open before him. I sat near the fire covered in furs, my eyes closed, and letting Tycho's beautifully spoken Latin drift past me like soft music.

Tycho stopped reading, paused a few seconds, and read again what even I could identify as the passage he had just completed. Then he paused again. I opened my eyes and looked towards him through the shadowy room. The boy was staring at Ahab who was gazing, distantly, at the ceiling. Tycho rose, leant across the table, and snapped his fingers at the tip of Ahab's nose. "Old father," the boy said. "Have you taken to sleeping with your eyes open?"

Ahab blinked, shook his head slightly, and sat up straight in his chair. Seeing Tycho leaning over the table towards him he said "Sit boy. Close your book."

"I'm curious about this *vessel of being* from the sky."

In lieu of a reply Ahab stood and paced slowly around the study. He paused at the window and looked at the wooden shutters, staring at them as though he were seeing through them a vision of the stars. He turned and moved towards the fire, ignoring me completely to stare at the dancing flames which cast a golden light onto his long dark gown and his aged bearded face. "Boy," he began, and from the tone of his voice I knew as well as Tycho that a lecture was forthcoming. "What do you make of your life?"

It was now Tycho's turn to respond to a question with silence. He shifted in his chair and, as though his eyes had suddenly begun to hurt from his reading, began to massage them forcefully with his hands. "We're about to speak of La Pucelle again," the boy said.

"It is important."

"She is important, yes. As to whether it is important for me to be given speeches about her, well, forgive me Ahab, but I think you're mistaken."

Ahab stood still before the fire, and though his back was now to the flames, there was enough light in the room for me to see the expression which came into his eyes when he spoke his next words. It was an expression of parental love, and his voice was hued with both pride and sadness. "Tycho, when compared to you, she is nothing."

"Please don't say that."

Ahab again began to pace, his hands clasped behind his back. "A peasant girl," he said, "most probably illiterate. She speaks only one language and before she met the Dauphin I can not imagine how she was able to comprehend the broader affairs of her country. Yet she saved her country."

"With God at her side, Ahab."

"But is that not speculation? If we consider the bare reality, we have a peasant girl inspiring despondent troops, devising plans of strategy, dictating courses of action to her monarch, all through the force of her will. With her will alone she has turned towards victory a war the French seemed to have all but lost.

"And then we have a youth named Tycho. An orphan with origins as inauspicious as Jeanne's, and yet who, whether by good fortune or talent, not only survived the bitterly harsh life of an orphan, but also travelled all over Christendom, learning dozens of languages and developing a story telling ability which is quite simply unparalleled anywhere in the known world. While the peasant girl is almost solely responsible for the salvation of her country, the wondrously talented boy wastes his gifts in the pursuit of tarts... "

"That's not true."

"And for the amusement of a Prince and Princess who...

"Whose father would gut and bury me unmarked somewhere if I ever tried to leave the city."

Again at the table, Ahab stared long and quietly at Tycho. He sat down, and the cold room sounded only with the crackling of the fire. Tycho idly traced figures on the wooden table before him. When he spoke he continued to look at his spiralling fingers, determined, it seemed, not to look into Ahab's eyes. "The comparison, as I have spoken before, is unfair. Jeanne is one of the heroes of the age. She is one, like Alexander, William of England, even Pawel, who has a fire burning within, a passion. She also has the advantage of having a cause - Ptolemy had geography, the Greeks had knowledge, you have the stars, Jeanne has her country. I have nothing. It would be..."

"Tycho, that is the crime. I have never met anyone, not even Pawel when he was young and leading troops back and forth across this country, who has the talent for inspiring others which you have. You merely have nothing to say."

"But that is the crux of my argument! I have not a cause and therefore all your discourse about my alleged talents is purposeless."

Ahab shook his head. "No," he said, and his voice seemed pleading with Tycho to believe him. "Something will occur. I will not believe that you'd be given your wondrous gifts merely to waste them in this sadly diseased castle. You'll be given something to say, you just can't be afraid to speak."

Tycho, who I'd never before seen angry, was approaching that emotion now. "I'm not afraid to speak!" the boy cried. "Your stars have neglected to provide me with something to say! You always cloak this fact, refusing to admit that it is the most important one!"

Ahab's lips parted but he resisted the temptation to speak. A look of sadness weighed upon him, as though conscious of having made a misstep in an incredibly weighty game. They didn't speak again, but stared at each other, the candles between them flickering in the chill drafts that chased through the room. Finally Tycho rose, collected his codex under his arm, and moved towards the door, his footsteps fading quickly in the winter darkness.

Ahab, sitting straight with his hands in his lap, was so still it was almost as though he slept. I watched him from beneath my fur, the fire burning beside me, and then I rose, expecting to follow Tycho, but Ahab's voice turned me from the door. "Do you understand, Samuel?"

The voice drifted through the darkened room more softly than a butterfly's ghost, yet it gripped me completely, leaving me wavering near the door.

"Samuel?"

But I did not comprehend the question. "Do I understand what, Ahab?"

"That Tycho must leave Gora."

"He'll be killed."

"That is not a certainty, but a risk, and one which must be accepted."

"The life in question is not your own Ahab."

"I know, but do you not sense it, Samuel, like an unexplained throb in your bones, that Tycho does not belong here, that something is amiss with the order of things?"

"Is that what your charts of the Heavens tell you?"

"No," and the word, spoken soft into the night, could not have been sadder. "It is ironic, but I am unable to locate upon my charts the life which I most desperately want to plot. I know only that within a year a great change shall occur in your life, and in Agnieszka's, and I assume that Tycho shall be involved, but the boy does not know the date of his birth, his very age is merely a guess, and my charts therefore tell me nothing of him."

"And how is it, if this be the case, that you are convinced he must leave Gora - from merely a throb in your bones?"

Ahab, after having long been staring at the fire, turned his head towards me. "But do you not feel it, Samuel?"

He was imploring me to agree with him, but I did not, and more hurtfully than I intended, I replied "I am a clown, Ahab. Ask me to sense in my bones if a joke is misworded, not if a boy should commit suicide."

I left him then, departing into the dark stone hallways, my words left behind to haunt Ahab as he sat in the glow of firelight in his wintry midnight room.

TONNELLI

JANUARY 1431

Colonna:

I have been reading of late, in Gora's marvellous library, about the Crusades. I found this from Humbert of Romanus; it is his answer to the question of the harm done to Christianity by having Christians dying in droves in foreign lands. I quote:

"The aim of Christianity is not to fill the earth, but to fill Heaven. Why should one worry if the number of Christians is lessened in the world by deaths endured for God? By this kind of death people make their way to Heaven who perhaps would never reach it by another road."

Odo, I have two thoughts upon this passage.

"A death endured for God." I can understand and sympathize with this. Indeed, those who are able to stand fast in their cause, though it means death, because of their faith in the Lord, have my utter and complete respect. I can think of hardly anything more noble than dying with a heart at ease because of your faith. But what of these horrible and pitiful lives endured for God? How can the poor of Christendom live their squalid lives believing it is God's will that they be poor and cold and famished and mere playthings at the whim of Kings? Why do they not rise in rebellion and carnage and attempt to improve their lives?

I can understand dying for God. I can not understand living like a rat for God.

My second thought is merely of the delicious irony. The implied "road to Heaven" which Humbert mentions. Is that not a wonderful Christian image? The souls of thousands of dead Crusaders tripping over the severed arms, shattered skulls, and slit throats of the people they'd slaughtered, people whose rotting corpses lie strewn across and along the road to Heaven.

Gieuseppi Tonnelli
Gora

BEAUVAIS

It had long been known, throughout the city, that a Knight from Burgundy was coming to woo Princess Alexandra. He arrived in mid January, and contrary to normal custom, he spent the first days of his stay in cheap lodgings in the Outer city, waiting until the day of his official reception before making his appearance at the castle.

When this day came, the Knight Beauvais, equipped in a suit of brilliant and shining armor, rode a magnificent stallion through the snowy streets of the city. Behind Beauvais marched pages with banners, and behind them four sturdy horses pulled a brilliantly bedecked carriage, driven by a man wearing, as did the pages, Beauvais's green and blue colours.

In the castle, as news of his approach spread, people began to race towards the seldom used but magnificent courtroom. This room is shaped as a square, and lying at one end there is a stage upon which sits the King's throne. The wall opposite the throne contains beautifully high windows. In two of the corners are spiral staircases which lead up to the galleries which line the walls between throne and windows. The courtroom is decorated in the red and while colours of Gora. The middle of the floor is covered in a thick red carpet, red and white banners hang over the gallery bannisters towards the floor, and more banners still are suspended from the wooden rafters of the ceiling.

The courtroom was near to bursting on the day of Beauvais's reception. The galleries brimmed with court members looking down upon events on the floor. The King, Krysztoff, the Countess, Ahab and others, stood on the stage upon which the throne rested. The center of the room was empty save for a small group of Burgundian men standing far on the opposite side of the room from the throne. All about the middle carpeted area, standing three or four people deep, waited the court spectators.

Agnieszka, Tycho and I stood amongst the observers to the right of Pawel's stage. We were fortunate to be at the front of the press of bodies, standing just off the cleared, carpeted area. It was not long before the first of the actors in the day's drama appeared - Beauvais entered the room to a frenzy of excited whispering. He bowed before Pawel and the Countess, and then crossed the room to stand with the small knot of his countrymen.

Beauvais was a tall man of perhaps twenty-five years. He was dressed entirely in gleaming silver armor, save for his head, which was uncovered. He had jet black hair which reached down to his shoulders, a beard less severely dark, green eyes, and he looked every bit the valiant warrior he'd been described as by the Countess.

The Countess had made Beauvais's life story well known in Gora. The man had dedicated himself to excellence in Knightly skills, and he had a program for training which made other Knights gape. He did somersaults fully armed and practiced jumping fully armed onto horseback. To practice siege skills he climbed a ladder wearing all his armor and using only his arms. When he removed his armor he could scale a ladder using only one hand. He also practiced scaling the narrow space between two walls using his back and feet. It was told that he could wrestle a wild horse to the ground by clenching tightly its mane and placing his other hand firmly between its ears.

And so, with this legendary Knight before us, his deeds and abilities being whispered about the room, Beauvais held our undivided attention. Until Alexandra arrived.

I think I have written that Alexandra is stunningly beautiful. Acquaintances who have travelled more than I tell me that she is perhaps among the ten most beautiful women on the continent, yet I have known her since her birth, and her beauty is something I have never been able to judge. I was shocked therefore, when Alexandra swept into the courtroom in a long flowing white dress, her golden hair loose about her shoulders, at Beauvais's reaction.

Upon Alexandra's entrance a cry sounded through the room which I can only describe as the whimpering scream of a man about to die from an excess of pleasure. Looking back towards Beauvais I saw the Knight with his armored arms extended towards the ceiling, beginning to scream in Flemish. Then he ran to Alexandra, who was standing in shock before the party on the raised stage, threw himself upon his knees at her feet, and began to shout passionately at her in French.

"Notre Seigneur, Que est aux cieux, vous nous avez beni avec un tel ange!"

Alexandra, who did not speak French, looked across the room to Tycho, who slipped from the crowd and crossed the red carpet to stand at the Princess's side.

"What does he say, Tycho?" Alexandra asked, staring wide eyed at the man exclaiming madly before her.

"Madame, votre beaute n'a pas de pareil...»

"He's jabbering about your beauty."

"Plus belle, plus brilliante, vous risquez la jalousie due soleil..."

"Jabbering."

"Que vos yeux soient au ciel, ils y seraient les etoiles les plus lumineuses..."

"That was nice."

"Je suis convaincu que vos mensonges meme ceux enrobes du miel, adouciraient les ames les plus amers... «

"Ehhh."

"Je vous rends, sans cesse, notre Seigneur la glorie pour votre naissance celeste! Ma Vie, madame, Ma Vie je placerais devant vous sur cette terre sacree!"

"Jabbering."

"Tycho!" Alexandra gasped, "he's beating his chest and tears are streaming from his eyes!"

"Aye?"

"Well translate him fully! Surely his words have more import than mere jabbering!"

"It is mostly jabbering, Princess. He is indeed engrossed with what he says, but it is all fairly mundane."

"Tycho, Tell Me!"

The boy looked softly at Alexandra, regarded Beauvais for a few seconds, the Knight still gushing nonsensically, and then turned back to the Princess. Their eyes met, and with the Burgundian at their feet and a score of people in the room, silence blossomed between them. I pushed away from Agnieszka, stepped across the carpet, and forgetting myself completely, took up position only paces from my two friends.

"Princess," Tycho began quietly, "the Knight is attempting to say that all the wonders are in your eyes. That a thousand springs could not fill his soul as does your smile. That you are so beautiful he wishes to die, here at your feet, to ensure that your visage is his last memory of life upon earth."

Alexandra, sixteen years of age, her blond hair falling past her shoulders, her blue eyes fixed on Tycho's face, did not respond. The two stared at each other for long minutes, oblivious to the hundred watching people, until Tycho seemed to grasp that a moment forbidden them was occurring. He swallowed slightly, shifted a foot, looked at me as I stared questioningly at him, and then turned to the still muttering Burgundian.

"My friend," he spoke in French, "the Princess is moved by your fervor, yet she doesn't have the French. She comprehends not a word you say. What other languages can you speak?"

His hands raised and clasped before him, his eyes closed, and his face tilted towards the ceiling, Beauvais, though no longer bellowing compliments, was now muttering complicated prayers to the Lord. He didn't respond or acknowledge Tycho's question, so the boy leant towards him and put his hand over the Burgundian's mouth. Beauvais's eyes opened and flashed quickly in anger. "Tremble lad," he hissed threateningly, "for if thou quit not my side I shall kill thee with a blade that has exited a hundred souls."

Tycho smiled. "My friend, the Princess comprehends you not. Your words are beautiful, but since they fall upon deaf ears you are merely presenting yourself as a bellowing madman. What other languages do you speak?"

Humbled slightly, Beauvais replied that he had German, English and Flemish. "Use German," Tycho advised him. "The Princess has German."

Beauvais snorted. "German! Are you insane! German is a tongue suited only for battles and brothels. My love for her can only be declared in French!"

After further argument Tycho finally persuaded the Knight to switch tongues. Rising, Beauvais stared into Alexandra's eyes. "Princess," he began, "it is only now that meaning has been imparted into my life. I pledge my soul and sword to your service. Your protector and defender shall I be."

"That's not..." Alex began, but Beauvais would not be stilled.

"Princess, never before have I felt as inspired as I now do. The Lord has struck me through the brilliance of your eyes. It shall be my honour, my destiny, to pledge my life to you. Beauvais shall be the name you cry when in peril, and, perhaps, it shall one day be the name you sigh when in love."

Alexandra stared long at Beauvais, who now stood with his head bowed to her. She turned to look at her father, who seemed unimpressed with the Knight's words, at the Countess who was smiling proudly, and then she turned again, looking into Beauvais's possessed eyes, then Tycho's amused ones. "Ah Tycho," she whispered.

TONNELLI

JANUARY 1431

Colonna:

A Knight from Burgundy, named Beauvais, arrived today at the castle. It has been predicted that he will wed Alexandra, and to mark their first meeting a lavish ceremony was held in the courtroom. In my opinion, Beauvais has already lost the Princess's hand by acting a Holy ass; an ass bent on chivalry and the Lord in a land where neither of these terms has meaning.

The drama of the Knight and the Princess, certain to dominate court gossip in coming weeks, came to be of only secondary importance to me today. In the courtroom, brimming with observers from castle and city, with the Knight prostrating himself before the Princess, I saw a woman, standing apart from the action, who caused a spectral shudder to hum within me. She is one of the childrens' favourites, their cook. Her name is Agnieszka.

The Princess of Gora, Alexandra, is a well celebrated beauty, and justly so, yet to my mind she is like a vision from dreams, an ethereal goddess who would be sullied by contact. She moves me to observe her, but not handle her.

Agnieszka's beauty is of the earth. I feel a man long at sea, desirous to toss myself upon her shore, embraced by her strength and comfort, mothered by her ample bosom. You know me, Odo, as a man easily fired, yet today, as I stared across the courtroom at this woman, I felt my lust to be a warning, as though, in my desire for her, I had seen a glimmer of my own destiny.

It is strange, Odo; an eerie presentiment. I feel as though pieces have been arranged on a board, and the first pawn has been moved.

Gieuseppi Tonnelli
Gora

TYCHO'S JOURNAL

FEBRUARY 1431

Jeanne began to hear voices at thirteen years of age - the voices of Saint Catherine, Margaret, and Michael. For five years she kept the voices secret, not telling others that she'd been bidden to save France. Then she rose to action, swayed Charles to her side and defeated the English.

And she's only eighteen years old. It is almost unbelievable - eighteen and already she has completed her mission from God.

Why her? In coming to a French girl does it mean God hates the English? If so, why does he not just sink their little island, deliver them a terrible outbreak of the plague, rather than destroy them through the unlikely route of speaking to a teenaged girl?

And, if rumours I've heard are correct, why does Jeanne's success doom her? I have spoken to the Countess and other visitors from French lands about Jeanne, and it seems, even now that she is in captivity, there is a plot led by the English, but assisted by the French church, to take her life. If she truly does hear the voices of the Saints, then her death must also be part of a higher plan, but does it not seem absurd? Raise a girl to national hero, and then have her killed by the church - won't that turn France against the Church? Is that what God wants?

Ahab feels that I am somehow related to Jeanne, that we are both recipients of some divine gift. And yet unlike Jeanne I have no mission. I weave stories to children in a castle. Ahab speaks as though my lack of purpose is my fault, but her mission came to Jeanne. The voices came to her and instructed her upon her course of action. Voices haven't come to me. God hasn't breathed a quest into my soul. Perhaps he wants nothing from me. Perhaps Gora and Alex and Krysz are my destiny.

But no. Ahab would clap his hands were I to tell him this, but I feel that there must be more.

Jeanne will die for her mission. Meanwhile I live safe and aimlessly. Which is better - to die for a cause or to live without one?

I do not wish to die, but if there is an afterlife, if fortune favours me with a journey to Heaven, and I am able to meet Dante and Petrarch, and they ask me "What did you make with your life?" I'd like to have an answer for them, other than an epic list of the women I'd pleasured; an answer of which I could be proud.

To die for a cause or to live without one?

How do you find your cause?

1435

I have Ahab's astrological charts. They are a jumble of scrolls which lie under my bed. I do not understand them and never look at them. Perhaps I should entrust them to the library, allow the scholars to care for them, rather than the cats who play in my room.

If someone asked Ahab to read his future, the old man would clear his desk of the papers and scrolls and knives and ink pots and overturned mugs, puddles of wax, year old ends of cheese - things which normally cluttered his work area, and unroll his charts upon the table, the ends secured beneath stones.

He would ask the person's year, month, date, and place of birth, and from this information plot the arrangement of the moon, sun and planets which had heralded his client into the world. He believed that the order of the spheres gave clues to a person's life, predicted, in general ways, the course of their life upon earth.

In the winter of 1431, what troubled Ahab most greatly about his charts was that Tycho was not upon them, and that something was amiss with the natural order of the world. I asked Ahab to explain the reasons for his concern to me, but of the barrage of planetary names and orbits which he spouted, all I can recall, all that I could comprehend, was the sorrow in his voice when he spoke of Venus, and the absolute hostility in his voice when he spoke of Mars - the warbling inconsistent orbit of which often left him hovering on the edge of despair.

I shall not, in this history, write much of Ahab, his charts and his Heavens, for I did not understand them. Yet they were important. They inspired Ahab to confront Tycho, often forcefully, about his talents and his future. He was convinced that the boy, mysteriously absent from his astronomical tables, was the key to the correction of what his charts described as a corruption in the natural order of the world.

What did he mean by natural world order? I don't know, but when he spoke of its corruption I believed him to be speaking of Gora, of the shadows cast upon it by Pawel's love.

11

THE VOICES

"Hush."

But the voices continued. They swept through the pitch of my bedroom like a thousand soft shushings of angels' wings. I repeated my request for silence, dreamily thinking that I lay with a girl who might heed me, but to no avail.

I opened my eyes and found that I was alone. The darkness rippled and eddied about me like billowing smoke. Voices, soft and feminine, whispered and sighed through the room. The words, save one, were inaudible, only waves of beautiful murmurs. The one word I could understand was "Tycho."

The midnight voices were whispering my name.

TONNELLI

FEBRUARY 1431

Colonna:

I have been much occupied of late with the fact that you are Christ's representative on earth. All through Christendom the uneducated shivering masses believe that in Rome, in your splendid church, you, and only you, are in direct contact with the saviour, conversing daily with him to receive his instructions.

Oh Pater

Consider this - at times in your life, when you have been on your knees, your Pope's robe pulled above your waist, your belly full of wine, sweat streaming from your brow, your hands full of some wench you've grabbed and wrestled to the floor, at moments like this, somewhere in the world, one of your sheep, one of Christ's children, is thinking "Perhaps Christ is talking to the glorious Martin right now."

Odo, when this idea first occurred to me... oh Lord, how I laughed....

I'm laughing now, I can't hold the quill, oh my stomach..

Gieuseppi Tonnelli
Gora

BEAUVAIS AND TYCHO

Tycho and I were well befuddled before we staggered into The Soldier's Inn, clutching each other to keep ourselves aloft. The boy was so sodden that he could no longer concentrate on a single story - every sentence he spoke reminded him of another tale, into which he'd lapse, and eventually such a confabulation of characters and events was in the air that the thread was gone, the listeners lost, and Tycho, sensing this, would silence himself

In The Soldier's Inn, which was bustling with noisy patrons, we had no sooner collapsed into chairs then a call went up for a story from Tycho. Two burly men lifted him onto a wooden table, but Tycho, his face whitening due to the upset the men had caused his stomach, clambered back down into his chair, where a large breasted country girl freed herself from the crowd and tossed herself into his lap.

"No, No," Tycho cried, waving a hand, which almost spilled the girl from his lap, at the crowd of people calling his name. "C'est impossible! I'm bloody soused already, a story from me now would only spoil our time!"

This only swelled the desire of the crowd. They began to pound their mugs against the tables. Tycho, realizing that an obliging woman was in his arms, momentarily forgot the crowd, kissed the maid, glanced up at the swell of cheering this caused and remembered what he'd been saying. "We must have another storyteller tonight!" he cried, squirming to keep his balance, which the maid in his lap was disrupting. This quieted the crowd somewhat and they began looking to each other, calling names, nudging friends in the ribs. My name was called, found wide acceptance, and others backed the call, but Tycho waved them down. "No," he called, "not

Samuel. We must have one of you tell a story, the jester and storyteller want only to listen tonight."

Out of the lull which ensued strode Beauvais.

While chanting Tycho's name, the crowd had created a small open space around the boy, and it was into this space that Beauvais walked, stopping before, and above, my friend.

Tycho at first did not recognize him. The Knight, who was now dressed plainly, likely only appeared to Tycho as a tall blur. With half his concentration directed upon the maid, Tycho looked up at Beauvais and said, cheerfully as a child, "Well met good sir! Have you a story for us?"

Towering over Tycho, Beauvais glared down upon him as though he were the most vile creature in existence. "You faithless promiscuous wretch..." he stammered, his mouth clenched nearly as tightly as his fists.

Lifting his face from the girl's, Tycho smiled drunkenly. "Well begun. I don't believe I know this story."

"Wasn't a story you criminal!" Beauvais raged, in Flemish, which left the majority of the spectators unable to follow the discussion. "How is it that I find you completely drunken, amidst this rabble, with this trollop in your arms?!"

Tycho stared confusedly up at Beauvais and then looked to me. "It's Beauvais," I told him. "The Countess's Knight from Burgundy. The Ma Vie je placerais devant vous bloke."

Tycho glanced up at Beauvais briefly, the Knight above him nearly apoplectic, and then back to me. "What is he on about?"

I shrugged. "Good sir," I called out, "does something trouble you?"

Beauvais turned to me, his mouth twitching in vexation. "His conduct," he said, pointing at the boy, "it is loathsome. He is dishonouring the Princess."

"The Princess?"

"The Princess! How am I dishonouring the Princess?"

"By dragging her love for you through this ditch of ale and whoring!" The Knight reached down and roughly grasped the arm of the girl in Tycho's lap. He pulled her from Tycho, tumbling her to the floor, and then pulled her to her feet and tossed her behind him into the stunned crowd. "Come," he said, motioning Tycho to rise. "You must quit this place."

Tycho rose, and as though Beauvais were as immaterial as a spirit, stepped through the Knight towards the maid who'd been wrenched from his lap. But Beauvais spun and clamped his hands upon Tycho's shoulders, hurling him back towards his chair, which Tycho hit and set clattering under the table.

With Tycho now lying on the floor, Beauvais stood above him, clenching, and unclenching his hands, searching for words. Unable to find his thoughts he muttered an almost inaudible apology, and turned to wade forcefully into the silent crowd. He disappeared out the door into the winter night.

Before I thought to move to help the boy, I saw his head appear above the edge of the table. He reached down and righted his chair, sat upon it, and looked to me across the table. "Beauvais believes the Princess loves me."

"Aye," I said. "He does."

The crowd began to revive. People stood above Tycho, clapping his shoulders, mussing his hair, while others stepped into the darkness to call abuse to the departed Knight. The maid who had been on Tycho's lap reclaimed her position, smiling sadly but proudly as though two men had battled over her, and while all this movement bubbled about us, Tycho grinned as though Beauvais's idea was sheer lunacy. I looked away from my friend and wondered from where the idea had come - was it a plot of the Countess's? An attempt to provoke Beauvais to great deeds through jealousy? Or was it simply the reception in the courtroom - when Alex had whispered "Ah Tycho..." softly, Beauvais bent before her?

TONNELLI

FEBRUARY 1431

Colonna:

In Gora, when people gossip about the city's luminaries, they discuss Pawel's despair, the ring which is NOT on Princess Alexandra's finger, and Prince Krysztoff's glowing potential as a King. Beyond the Royal Family there are two other names which are mentioned often in conversation.

The city's scholars discuss Ahab and the old man's theories upon the stars, medicine, magnetism, whatever he has studied of late.

The other name, which daily rings like a small clear bell in homes and shops and inns about the city, is Tycho. Tycho is a lad of sixteen or seventeen years, whose fame rests upon two things - he is the court storyteller, possessing an unnatural talent for creating tales which, even after having been passed from friend to friend across the city, bring imaginary lands vividly to the mind, make hearts ache for the sorrows of fabulous beings.

The second reason for the boy's fame is that he has slept, or so it is said, with every woman in Gora. Obviously this is impossible, but it is undoubtedly true that he has slept with the beauties of every class - from the preening wives of court officials, to the maids of the flea infested inns of the city. Interesting as well is that far from being shunned, his sexual proclivity actually makes him respected and desired.

I spoke today, for the first time, with this boy. He came to me while I was hearing confessions, and I write to you of this encounter for it has left me vaguely shaken. Through the grill, a young bubbling voice gushed, "Bishop Tonnelli? This is Tycho, the storyteller."

"Tycho!" I exclaimed. "You want to confess!"

"Confess! No, I wish to speak with you."

"We cannot speak here."

"People always speak here, is that not what the confessional is for?"

"The confessional is for freedom from sin, child. It is a sacred place; we can't discuss weather and women here."

"Shall we go to an inn?"

"What is it Tycho, that you wish to speak with me about?"

"Saints."

"Saints?"

"Aye."

"What of them?"

The gushing child disappeared now Odo, and a soft, concerned voice came to me through the grill. "Tonnelli, I often hear of people, of no exceptional note, who begin to hear the voices of the saints, or to see visions. I fear... Tonnelli, have the saints ever spoken to you?"

"No child," I replied, growing intensely curious. "The Saints do not communicate with me."

"Do you think, and I vow that I'm not jesting, can it be possible, that when the saints speak to a person, can it be erotic?"

"Erotic?'

"Tonnelli, voices whisper to me when I sleep. As of yet it is all babble, incoherent sounds, but they wake me, refuse me rest. I fear that I am unable to understand only because they speak a language, a language of deathly whispers, which I've not yet learnt, but each night I fear that I may come to understand their words, that I may one day have to listen to what they say.

"The voices are female. There are at least two, perhaps more, and lying in bed I am frozen by two separate emotions - I feel someone, or something, has been trying desperately to communicate with me, but also I'm aroused. Female voices whispering softly in my dreams all night, as you can imagine, I wake with an erection the size of.."

"Yes, yes," I interrupted. I paused for a few moments, my mind racing, and then simply asked why he had come to me. His answer was long in coming, and when he again spoke his voice trembled, as though fearful. "Bishop Tonnelli," he whispered, and such was my desire to hear him that I pressed close to the metal grill, "despite what some speak of you, you are a man of the Lord. I assume you are impressively versed in Christian thought and writing. I need to know if Saints have revealed themselves to others as I've described the voices which visit me, or, alternatively, if what I have told you rings of madness."

And you Odo?

How would you have responded to this boy, of whom so much is spoken, whose conversation was conducted in an exquisite Latin, whose voice trembled through the fear that he was indeed being approached by the Saints?

I gave him banalities, Odo. I told him of the Lord's seeming delight in cloaking symbols with mystery, and I warned him of Satan's delight in imitating the Lord to lead astray God's children. When the boy left I lingered alone in the enclosed space of the confessional, staring at the small wooden cross which I had long ago hung upon the inside of the door.

Despite my words, my advice that the boy's dreams were only delusions, I felt fear.

The boy's words had implied a knowledge of my sins, and though this should make me fearful, the true reason for my fear was the growing certainty that the story teller's dreams were more dangerous than madness. I have lived in this Godless land a long while, and the thought that the Lord has taken an interest in a life close to mine leads me to wonder if my time of judgment is soon to come.

Gieuseppi Tonnelli
Gora

TYCHO'S JOURNAL

FEBRUARY 1431

I woke to the sound of pages turning, the rustling of paper. Ahab was sitting at my desk, almost invisible so much did he blend into the grey morning light. He was flipping idly through one of the volumes of my Bible. I watched him a short while, then announced that I was awake by mumbling "Good Morning."

Ahab closed my Bible and without any preamble presented me with a riddle.

Two men.

Josef was a prisoner in a dank underground cell and would be for the rest of his life. He ate crusts of bread when lucky enough to be fed, drank filthy water, endured beatings and fell asleep listening to rats scurrying around him. Josef's life was spent in the dark shadow of misery, but every day, for one hour, Josef's wife, who loved him deeply, came to his cell and they talked freely together through a narrow metal grill.

In his life of darkness, Josef had one hour a day with his wife.

Stanislaw was a farmer. Thirty years old. His parents were dead, he had no siblings, and having never married he had no children. For a farmer he was wealthy, having money saved to last him two poor harvests, a fortune. Stanislaw had money and as much as possible in this world he was free. But he was alone. When he was sick no one was near to care, and when he died, when he was lowered into the earth, no one would ever visit his stone.

Josef would always be in prison. Stanislaw would always be alone.

"My question," Ahab asked, a specter in the wintry morning light, possibly even an apparition from my recently twisted dreams, "is which of these men would you rather be? Which life would you choose?"

I lay staring at the ceiling, the blankets and covers pulled to my chin. "You're asking me which is more important - love or freedom?"

Ahab nodded.

I closed my eyes.

1435

A year ago, when I first read Tonnelli's letter concerning his meeting with Tycho in the confessional, it surprised me greatly.

I read Tycho's journal before beginning on Tonnelli's letters, and so I knew of the voices which interrupted the boy's nights. In the journal the voices are mentioned merely once or twice, and never in terms which suggest that they greatly disturbed him. Yet if he felt a need to discuss the voices with Tonnelli, who he had never met, and who he would have heard, for two years, be described in only the foulest of terms, they must have disturbed him much more than was evident in his journal.

I am surprised as well by the effect which Tycho had upon Tonnelli. I had long known that Ahab felt Tycho to be some manner of prodigy, and apparently, after a single conversation, Tonnelli felt this way as well. "The storyteller's dreams are more dangerous than madness." It is an intriguing statement, and it leads me to wonder what Tonnelli suspected. Did he truly think that Tycho's dreams were evidence of the Lord taking notice of Gora? And was this, for Tonnelli, something to welcome or to fear? For he wrote often, and with certainty, of one day being punished for his sins.

The meeting between Tycho and Tonnelli also stirs me personally. I find myself oddly delighted in imagining these two speaking together in the confessional, separated by only the thinnest of walls, when I'd previously believed that they had only met for a few frantic moments on the night of the escape.

Although I envied him desperately, Tycho was my friend. He brought life to this dark castle even before the great sacrifice which ended his time here. I feel indebted to

Tycho, but also I feel indebted to Tonnelli. As a dwarf and a Christian, I am a freak in Gora. I have always been a freak and am accustomed to it, yet it is a savagely lonely life.

The Bishop was a freak in much the same manner as I, and I felt a kinship with him - where I am a dwarf he was grotesquely fat, and we were both Christians, or at least I was. From his letters it is apparent that by 1431 Tonnelli had grown rabidly anti Catholic, and may only nominally have been a Christian, but he manifested himself as one. I was able to take strength from the faith which I imagined lay within him. I also took strength from his obesity - for he had the courage, or perhaps the pompousness, to be indifferent as to how others viewed him - a lesson, regarding my height that I had never truly learnt.

And so I am delighted to know that these two actually met, and spoke, prior to the few seconds when they confronted each other on the night of the escape, when both would have had good reason to believe that they were rushing headlong into the arms of death.

12

KRISTINA

AGNIESZKA AND MICHAL

I lifted several wooden blocks from the floor and sent them swirling into the air. Tycho played with the fire, the prince dozed, Alexandra and Agnieszka chatted softly in the still room. Intent on my juggling, my eyes upon the dim twirling shadows the blocks cast upon the ceiling above, I listened only distantly to the girls' conversation. I stepped idly through the shadowy room, my hands in motion, my mind clear, until I heard Tycho's voice interrupting the girls.

"Tell her the ending."

The boy's voice quieted Agnes and Alex. I caught the blocks in my palms and fingers and in the curves of my wrists, then allowed them to tumble to the floor. I looked towards Agnieszka and Alexandra, who were staring at Tycho. "Perhaps," Agnieszka said, her eyes upon the boy, "you should tell the ending."

He eased away from the fire, touched my shoulders, impelling me towards my chair near the bed. He touched Krysztoff's shoulder and whispered to the sleeping prince that a second story was to be told. Krysz rubbed his eyes, sat up beside his sister, and asked "What story will you tell?"

Tycho smiled down at him, then looked across at Agnieszka sitting on the other side of the bed. The smile on his face faded, and after a long moment's pause, in a voice soft and barely audible, he answered "The story of Agnieszka and Michal. Close your eyes."

I wish it were possible to simply copy into this history the tale which Tycho graced us with that night, but it does not appear in Ahab's ledger. I think the old man retired upon the completion of Tycho's first story. As for my memory, I have nuances and echoes, but not the entire text, not enough to be worthy of the story's sad beauty.

It was a story we all knew - that of Agnieszka's hasty marriage prior to being escorted to Gora by Pawel's emissary and soldiers. A story we all knew, so perhaps it was Tycho's shading which moved us - Agnieszka and Michal saying their parting words beside a tree which many years ago, when they were children, they had together watched be struck by lightning. The twenty mounted men of the escort softly cooing to their horses as Agnieszka said her final words, and then stepped away from her husband. She raised herself high atop a waiting horse, and then horse after horse began stepping slowly away, Agnes staring over her shoulder as Michal, standing motionless with the houses of Kozle behind him, became only a shadow on the landscape. She whispered his name, and as she did, his shadow faded into a goodbye.

When I opened my eyes, long after Tycho's voice had gone still, I found the Prince staring vaguely past me towards the fire, the Princess looking softly towards her friend, and

Agnieszka sitting motionless with her eyes closed. Tycho was gone.

I murmured goodnight and left, rushing to the boy's room. I pushed the fur aside to see Tycho seated at his desk, a single wavering candle burning before him. "Tycho," I gasped, slightly out of breath, "how did you know, so perfectly, of Agnieszka's parting?"

In a soft voice, his gaze fixed upon the candle, he replied "How do I ever know?"

The succeeding moments in that room were long and awkward. I knew not what to say, and had almost decided to leave, when Tycho spoke my name. "Sam," he said, "when she learns the truth, Agnieszka will attempt an escape, won't she?"

"I believe so."

"Should we try to sway her from this?"

"You know how strong headed she is, she would never heed us."

"She'll die."

I stepped towards Tycho's desk, reaching out in the darkness to find his second chair. I sat down, the candle between us, and looked through the dim light towards my friend. "Tycho, Agnes may be intelligent, and fortunate enough, to find a way through the Barbican and into the outer city. It will be difficult, but in this great city there must be a way. The obstacle is not so much the Barbican as it is the flight to Kozle.

"In escaping Pawel she will need to walk for days and nights in a straight line towards her home. She will have to survive thieves and wolves in the forests, find shelter, and food, and water, all of this while Pawel's soldiers pursue her. Agnes could never do this Tycho, she still becomes lost in this castle, and aside from her trip to Gora, she has never left her

village. Agnes could never find her way to Kozle, but you can.
- if the two of you left together... "

The words trailed away from me. Tycho remained
silent, perhaps shaken by what I had implied. I watched him
for a few moments; he stared at the candle flame, his face
impassive, and believing that I had said enough on this night,
I rose and left him.

TONNELLI

FEBRUARY 1431

Colonna:

It is past midnight in this bitterly cold land. I have stirred the embers in my hearth, laid scraps of kindling upon the coals, and am praying for a blaze to begin. I crave warmth and company on this night, if only that provided by fire, for I've been awoken by yet another nightmare.

In complete darkness I am stumbling up the crumbling steps of a high tower. I trail my left hand upon the wall and wave my right before me, deflecting ghosts, collecting cobwebs, searching for bats' nests, hanging corpses, lethal traps and devices.

When it seems I have reached the summit of the tower, if I were to move outside I'd enter a roiling midnight cloud, a stair crumbles away beneath my foot. I am left tottering in the darkness, flailing my arms in a desperate attempt to find a handhold which will rescue me from a long deathly fall. Panicking, my hand touches something hanging above me in the darkness. I reach again and grasp a tangle of ropes which jerk mightily with my sudden weight. Close above me bells begin to toll, more powerful and thundering than all the bells of Rome chiming on Christmas morning.

The echo of the bells stretches through the night, reaches across the width and breadth of Christendom. The bells cause people to gather in the streets of villages and cities, rubbing their eyes, staring towards the stars, towards Heaven, wondering why the bells had sounded, what message lay within their chime.

In my black tower I am near death. I kick my feet, frantically searching for a foothold, but none is there. Soon my arms and grip will weaken, and the ropes will slide from my grasp. I will fall into the cold dark arms of an abyss. I shall fall forever, but expect death every second - the Hell chosen for me by the Lord.

Such is my nightmare, and perhaps it less frightens than intrigues me. I have long expected a horrible death, a death occurring beyond the reach of God's mercy, and so the fate prophesied me by my dream does not surprise me.

It is the bells, Odo, the idea that I shall somehow rouse Christendom. My life has been one of darkness rather than light, but perhaps my death shall have meaning - perhaps my death will cause waves which even you, barricaded behind your wealth and power, shall feel in Rome.

Gieuseppi Tonnelli
Gora

TYCHO'S JOURNAL

FEBRUARY 1431

The hand upon my shoulder was rough and insistent, and though it was shaking me from sleep I was little vexed, for I thought merely that the girl I was with wanted me for pleasure. A horror it was then to open my eyes and see Beauvais.

My fear was that he had woken me so that he could pledge, in all honesty, that he hadn't slain me in my sleep. But Beauvais, after waking me, moved off from my bed, unlatched the shutters of my window, and opened them to admit a rush of shivering air and the grey light of early morning.

He looked out across the city, towards the distant countryside. "It has not failed me to notice the high regard in which you are held by the Princess," he said, staring softly through the window. "At first I was furious - a lustful whelp, a counterfeiter of love such as yourself, holding in your hand the love of the most splendid woman on earth."

"Beauvais..."

He waved a finger to silence me. "In my land, the proofs of love are deeds, and actions. It is with these tools that I shall defeat you."

"Defeat me?"

"I have in mind an act which will allow me to eclipse you for Alexandra's affections."

"Beauvais, your belief that I am a rival to you for the Princess is a mistaken one..."

"Storyteller, stop prattling. I woke you to inform you of my plan. I shall not enter into a debate with you."

The look upon his face was of a dog's sadness, and though anxious to relieve him of his mistaken belief that the

Princess loved me, I stilled myself. I sat silently in my bed, shivering due to the rush of cold air blowing through the room. "I have in mind a vigil," Beauvais said. "I shall defend the bridge over the Ardo river, for an entire week, against any man who wishes to challenge me for Alexandra's love."

Defend the bridge? "I don't understand."

The look in his eyes was now one of pity, as though he spoke of deeds the glory and honour of which I could never comprehend. "Certainly you do not understand," he said.

"You vow to defend the bridge. Against whom? Have you intelligence of an attack upon the bridge?"

The Knight shook his head, growing slightly exasperated. "It was a figure of speech. I shall wait, for one week, upon the bridge. If any man wishes to lay claim to Alexandra's hand he will have to joust against me upon the bridge. If defeated I will retire gracefully, but I shall not be defeated."

"When will this occur? Spring?"

"I shall attend Mass on Sunday and begin my vigil the next day."

"This coming Monday?"

"Aye."

"And what shall you do then, ride from your lodgings in the city each morning, down to the bridge, and then return to your lodgings at sunset?"

"Even a stripling such as yourself could accomplish that. No, I shall remain upon the bridge, unmoving, for the entire week."

I stared long at the poor man, unable to believe that he was serious. "Beauvais, surely you have taken note of the temperature outside. To do as you plan, it is suicide."

The Knight turned towards the window, the view of snowy wastes encircling the city. "Death for a lady," he mused, quietly, and then he again turned his face towards mine and

I felt a pitiable wretch, shivering amongst my furs, while he stood unflinching in the icy draughts sweeping into the room. "Storyteller," he said, and all traces of the man I'd laughed at in the courtroom, and the man who'd tossed me to the floor in the alehouse, were gone, "Storyteller, is such a death worthy?"

"Beauvais... who am I to answer such a question?"

"You are the one who is loved by Alexandra."

"No, I am not."

He smiled at my denial, and a moment later eased himself from the window. "Promise me, storyteller, that you shall at least visit me upon the bridge."

"I shall."

He nodded to me, his eyes soft, thankful, and touched his hand to my hanging fur. "That is well then, I thank you. Farewell storyteller."

Is such a death worthy? Ahab would be curious to know my answer to this question, and yet I do not have one. Perhaps this should distress me, but more I find myself thinking of Beauvais - he doubts himself, yet is prepared to die for Alexandra.

And I?

TYCHO'S JOURNAL

FEBRUARY 1431

I was asleep upon my desk, my head lying on my Bible, when a chill struck my shoulder, waking me. I rose in my chair, touched my fingers to my eyes and glanced about the room. The window was shuttered, all was black. I could see nothing.

I reached across my desk, attempting to find a candle which I would light at a torch in the hall, but as I searched, I felt fingers touch my hand.

I froze in my chair, aware now that the chill which had awoken me had been an otherworldly presence entering my room. My eyes, as I sat rooted in my chair, grew accustomed to the darkness - murky shapes began to appear, and I saw her.

She was sitting upon my bed, her legs dangling over the edge, her hands in her lap.

It is true what people say, Alexandra is the living image of her mother.

Kristina smiled and raised her hands towards me. I moved to her, sat beside her on the bed. She put an arm about my shoulders, reached her other hand across her body and touched my arm. I turned my face into her shoulder, into her long golden hair. She touched her fingers to my cheek, kissed the top of my head, held me close, and whispered my name. "Tycho," she said, the voice from my dreams, the voice I had come to fear.

THE FUTURE

The winter of 1431 was one of the most severe in memory. I have, in my life, often envied the lands about the Mediterranean, where it is warm all year and winter simply requires an extra blanket on the bed. In Gora, especially in 1431, winter meant death - food is scarce, clothing is never warm nor thick enough, and the poor sit staring at their fires, shaking, pondering which piece of furniture to burn next.

I still remember, twenty years later, winters in Cologne with my parents and brother - how we shivered together in bed, the fragile bubble of warmth created by our bodies holding back an ocean of freezing night. I would lie between my brother and parents staring up into the darkness, seeing Death himself, bony skull dully visible within the dark folds of his hood and cloak, plying with his hands across the delicate surface of our warmth, searching for an entrance, and searching patiently, knowing well that he could return again if we managed to survive his prickings that night.

A stretch of weeks fell in February 1431, when, despite my insomnia, the nights were too cold for wandering. I remained in my room through all those dark midnight hours, staring into my fire, praying either for sleep or warmth. One night, while I sat denied of both these gifts, there came a rapping upon my door. Tycho, who I'd jealously expected to be lying warm between the bodies of two or three women, entered and nodded wordlessly to me.

He moved to my bed and sat down, his legs hanging over the edge.

He asked if Ahab was capable of entering, or crafting, peoples' dreams. Surprised, I replied "Tycho, why?"

He rubbed his palms into his eyes, then lay down upon my bed, tugging a fur across his chest. "Samuel," he said, his voice merely a hush in the shadows of my room, the silence of the castle, "I have, for over a month, heard voices in my dreams."

"What do they speak?"

"Nothing. They merely swirl and shush, and when they do speak clearly it is simply to whisper my name. I have become afraid of sleep, afraid that the voices will be similar to those of Jeanne's and begin to demand something of me."

"And you suspect that the voices are sent to you by Ahab?"

"I thought it a possibility."

"Do not. In other kingdoms, what you have said would result in Ahab being burnt as a sorcerer."

The boy shifted from his back to his side, tugging the fur closer about him, looking out over the room, towards me, towards the fire. "What of Kristina?"

"Kristina?"

"Has it ever been suspected that she is not merely a phantom of Pawel's madness? Have any others in the castle seen her?"

"I have seen her."

The boy's eyes, which had been growing sleepy, flickered to life and he stared at me for long moments, but he did not question me further. I turned from my friend's dark form to stare at the fire. A long stretch of silence gripped us, and just when I thought he had fallen asleep, Tycho began to speak again, but his voice was distant, as though the winter winds which sounded outside the castle had wrapped about him, and he was calmly whispering to me through their embrace.

"Samuel, for years I'll be alone. I'll be the beggar I was as a child, sleeping in trees, wading through rivers, my only companion my shadow - a faint and mute ghost bobbing behind, or beside, or before me.

"I'll walk through Christendom alone, for years, and then, when the strength of my youth is no longer within my bones, I'll be lost in a winter storm. My legs knee deep in snow, the air about me a whirlwind of flakes, I will tumble and fall, my body burying into the whiteness. The winter will rage about me, smoothing a cold blanket over me, and cold and unloved, far from every friend I've ever known, I'll die.

"That is what is being asked of me, Sam. Ahab employs words like destiny and responsibility, and Agnes deserves to be freed from Pawel, to be reunited with her husband, but if I rise to stretch out my arms as Ahab desires, I shall die alone, that terrible unmourned death which haunts the dreams of travelers."

He lay on my bed through the night. He did not move, or speak, until dawn, when he rose and stepped from my room. I had no comforting words to give him. I have been a traveller and I know that dream, and I felt, sorrowfully, that Tycho had already foreseen this death, that he had learned from Ahab the art of reading the stars.

1435

"It was me."

In Tycho's room, my writing room, after returning the scroll of my latest scribblings, Alexandra sat quietly upon Tycho's bed, the candlelight catching in her golden hair. I sat at the desk for long moments, aware that she had spoken something of great consequence, but not understanding to what she had referred.

"Princess?"

She looked down at the bed, and thanks to the several candles, I was able to discern a faint smile upon her lips. "Exactly here," she said, patting her hand on the bed beside her. "How many years past, Samuel? I sat here, with Tycho in my arms, knowing as I held him that he believed me to be my mother's ghost."

I am only now, hours later, recovering from the shock of my conversation with Alexandra. Beauvais had been correct, she had indeed loved Tycho.

"But why..." I stammered, unable to shape the tumult of my thoughts into words.

"Samuel," she answered, anticipating my question, "I could not have spoken of my feelings. What would it have done to our small family if all knew I was harbouring an unrequited love for Tycho? What would it have done to Tycho? He would have been cast into such confusion...," she paused a few seconds, then simply smiled to me through the candlelight. "You knew Tycho," she said. "Do you think he could have been at peace with me if I'd spoken to him the word love?"

"But Alexandra!" I gasped, becoming excited, "everything may have changed! He may have stayed! He may have found some other way..."

"He did not love me, Samuel. I knew that even when I longed for him most desperately, as on the night I came to his room merely to touch his hair, and ended the night playing the part of my mother's ghost while he wept upon my shoulder."

She spoke other things, ideas I do not yet grasp and shall need to ponder in coming days. She said that Tycho's heart was not made for love. I answered that this was cruel, but she shook her head. "Not cruel simply sad, and though sad it is true."

Perhaps.

She said as well that she still loved him.

This castle, this Kingdom.

13

THE BRIDGE

TYCHO'S JOURNAL

MARCH 1431

The Countess kissed me, her tongue slowly exploring my mouth in gentle strokes of movement. Finally I stepped away, bowed slightly, smiling at the satiated lust in her eyes, and backed out the door.

It was late morning. The night had been one of adventure, the morning full of half dreamt caresses. I intended to make for my room and sleep away the day, but it was not to be. In winter, when the castle's windows are shuttered to the cold, the halls resemble subterranean passages, lit only dimly by torches on the walls. Yet sometimes, such as on this morning, the light of day manages to seep through a thousand crevices and give a murky light, such as that underwater, to the castle.

Alexandra - and I was only paces away from the Countess's door when she appeared - was moving towards me through this misty light. I fleetingly thought that this was again Kristina, but as she moved closer I saw the smile upon the face, heard my name exclaimed in delight, and I felt a real and warm hand grasp my arm. "Tycho!" she said, her blue eyes shining, "where are you going?" I told her that I was for my room, but with her hand upon my arm she returned me to the Countess's door, upon which she knocked. "This is fortunate," she said. "You can assist me. We must convince the Countess to sway Beauvais from his vigil."

We were met politely but with some surprise. The Countess's eyes lingered amusedly upon mine as I followed Alexandra into the room. Unclothed when I had left her moments before, the Countess now wore a blue nightdress, her long blond hair loose and spilling freely over her shoulders, down her back. We were led to chairs near the fire, the Countess brought us furs for warmth, she discreetly closed the curtains about the disheveled bed, and when she sat down with us at the fire, a fur draped about her, Alexandra stated her plea for the Countess to turn Beauvais from his suicidal vigil.

The Countess gazed steadily at the Princess. The fire crackled brightly beside her, and after a few moments of thought, her reply was, "You don't understand love."

For the next hour I attempted to stay a part of the conversation, but circumstances were against me. The fire and fur gave warmth to my weary body, the chair was well cushioned, two of the most beautiful women in my life were before me, bathed in firelight, and often I dozed.

The conversation was one which interested me only slightly. The love the Countess spoke of was known to me from a hundred stories - stories in which a Knight strives to prove himself worthy of a lady he can never have, often because she is already married.

The Knight battles sorcerers, resists sirens, slays dragons, all in the hope of raising himself in the esteem of his lady. I have always thought that this manner of love was one of fiction only- a device used to give impetus to a story, but the Countess declared that this was the love Beauvais held for the Princess. I do not know if she is correct. Something indeed is propelling Beauvais towards death, but whether it is Alexandra alone...

Alexandra was similarly convinced that death would be Beauvais's reward for his vigil, but the Countess, deaf to Alex's arguments, refused to believe that she would lose her Knight. "Princess," she answered, smiling patiently, "the truth of love is that it is better to hope for, rather than to have, the beloved. Beauvais has recognized you as a lady far above him in birth and virtue. He knows that he can never attain you, and yet he will attempt glorious and honourable deeds, such as this defense of the bridge, in order to rise in honour and virtue until he is worthy of you."

Alexandra shook her head in vexation. "This is mere philosophizing," she said, "and events require action. It is as though a man stood before us with a blade to his throat, threatening to spill his own blood, while we casually discussed the events in his life which had led him to suicide. Beauvais shall die upon the bridge, yet you defend him... for what reason? The fear of failing in your mission for Philip The Good?"

"He will not die."

"He will die!" Alex turned to me, her voice rough with frustration. "Tycho?"

"Countess, the Princess is correct. A week in this weather is not possible."

She observed Alexandra and I for a short while, her brows knit in thought. She pushed back in her chair, staring into the fire with her fur clutched about her. "The impasse between us," she began, "lies in our conception of love, and I do not think this impasse can be easily resolved, for you seem to regard me as a being from some distant continent with outlandish morals and customs, but let me speak it thus - Princess, at this moment, you are the pinnacle of Beauvais's desires. He well knows himself to be unworthy of you, yet in striving to be worthy of you he will improve himself as a Knight, as a soldier of God. How then can you ask me to turn him from this path? It is one which will raise him in the eyes of men and attain for him a place in Heaven."

Alexandra slumped in her chair. They had spoken, and argued, a long while, and she seemed exhausted. "He will be in Heaven very shortly," she murmured.

TYCHO'S JOURNAL

MARCH 1431

After my story last night, Agnieszka and I walked together through the castle, through the dark, echoing stone passages, and eventually found ourselves in the dining hall.

It was black and empty, and for several moments we simply stood near the entrance, listening to our whispers scurry off into the murky emptiness. I took Agnieszka's hand and guided her through the maze of invisible tables towards one of the fireplaces. I set her down in a chair, ran back to the hallway and brought a torch flaming before me into the room. With much effort I built a fire, fueling it with wood until it was high and warm, and Agnieszka and I sat in chairs before the fire, a great darkness above and around us, warm furs clutched tightly about our shoulders.

We spoke lazily, allowing lulls to exist in our conversation - long lulls when we sat listening to the crackling of the flames, content with silence, perhaps even comforted by it.

I asked her to explain how she felt for her husband.

The question turned her face to mine. "I love him, Tycho."

"But love, Agnieszka, this word, I want to know what you mean by it."

Her beautiful eyes, harbouring a reflection of the fire, turned from me. In her silence I realized that she was struggling, for the first time, to put a true meaning to this word. I closed my eyes, enjoyed the glow and warmth of the fire upon my face, leant back into the embrace of the night.

"He makes me happy."

"I make you happy, as does cooking, and you would not use this word for us."

"I would," she replied. "I love cooking, and I love you, in a way."

"It is not the same."

"No," she said, gazing into the flames. "No. It is a different manner of love." She told me how, after all these months, she could still feel the touch of his hand, could close her eyes and count, from memory, the number of wrinkles upon his forehead when he frowned. She spoke of the strength and warmth of his arms, how she could endure anything if she knew he was awaiting her, and how this separation, caused by Pawel's money, had caused a gnawing ache within her, affecting her so deeply at times that she merely wished to lay curled in bed, too weak to stand.

So, when Agnieszka says "I love my husband," this is what she means.

After a long silence, Agnes turned the conversation to me. I deflected her a few times, a game I like to play with her - she asks questions and I reply with non sequiturs which enrage her, but finally, and in exasperation, she said "You've never been in love, have you?"

It was no secret; in fact I may even have told her as much before. I paused for a long while, staring at the fire, and then let slip an idea I'd long kept to myself, fearing to speak it, as though utterance would make it true. "My heart," I whispered, "seems not designed for love."

She was staring at me. "Tycho, I love you. I have told you as much."

The firelight was shining upon her face, in her eyes, across her long brown hair. I dropped my eyes from hers to look again into the fire, burning bravely in the vast darkness of the dining hall. "It is not the kind of love which can save me. Not the kind of love that will save me from the storm."

She didn't reply, my words stilling her, and after sitting long and silently by the fire, I guided Agnes to her room.

I feel strongly for Agnieszka, and perhaps it is love that I feel, but I long thought that the emotion which inspired Petrarch and Dante to write all those words for Laura and Beatrice, and which allowed Abelard to endure castration for Eloise, would be much different, and somehow allied to sex.

I wish Petrarch's spirit would visit me in my cold room. I would like to ask him what he would do - knowing that Agnieszka loves a man she is being kept from, what would you do? Is love so beautiful and precious a thing that you would sacrifice your life to it, though the love be not your own?

I wish you could tell me Petrarch. I do not know or feel love. I believe in love, and not only because of you and Dante and Abelard, but also because I can see it in Agnieszka. When she thinks of her husband something shines through her. She becomes distant, and strong, and weak. The emotions she holds for Michal could protect her against the coldest night, but somehow she also seems vulnerable, as though she would die if anything happened to her husband.

That, I presume, is love.

I believe in love.

I don't understand love.

Agnieszka is my friend.

I'm happy in Gora. I have a family here, and the thought of returning to the life I knew as a child - nights under open skies, praying in the early morning hours for sleep to return, even the sleep of death, so that I'll no longer feel the cold, terrifies me.

But this love, Agnieszka's manner of love, seems to be a very rare thing.

THE BRIDGE

The river was frozen, the trees of the forest beyond were bare, spindly limbs stretching into the grey sky. Beauvais was alone, atop his stallion. Flakes of snow, gathered by the wind, swept about him, racing over the river ice in bitter puffs.

I have been kin to loneliness all my life, but Beauvais, on that harsh winter day, was the most forlorn being I have ever seen, and contrary to my previous indifference, my heart ached for him.

Alexandra, Tycho and I, with a small party of guards behind us, walked halfway onto the bridge. We gazed a long while upon the horse and armored rider. Beauvais's mount was a magnificent brown beast. It stood with its head slightly lowered, gusts of breath exiting its nostrils sadly, and slowly. On either side of horse and rider the sides of the bridge swept up in short, snow topped walls, reaching roughly the height of the horse's belly.

Alexandra, in a fur hat and long winter coat, moved ahead of us. She stopped before the lowered head of the horse, removed a hand from her muffler to pet, briefly, the star of white hair upon the beast's nose. She looked up at Beauvais, whose visor was down, thereby entirely shielding the man inside from view. He was a suit of silver metal, and I can not imagine how cold he was, how blue he would have been had we seen his face.

"Good Knight," Alexandra said. "I appreciate that you wish to pledge yourself to me. It is a noble and chivalrous gift, and I thank you for considering me worthy of your service. Yet I cannot accept. This is not done in my land. Noble ladies do not collect Knights who parade about until her honour requires defending. I shall never love you, and therefore this act is both unnecessary and inappropriate. I also fear that

192

you will not survive, and I do not wish your death upon my conscience."

Far away the branches of trees rubbed together in the wind, and this distant rustling of wood was the only sound to follow Alexandra's speech. Beauvais's horse dipped its head lower towards the ground. Finally a voice rumbled hollowly out of the suit of armor above Alexandra.

"Princess," the voice began, "to simply state my love for you would not, I suspect, turn your heart towards me. In fact that is perhaps an inadequate way to express the emotions within me, for I find that I do not desire your hand in marriage. Indeed, I feel that it would be sacrilege for you to associate so closely with one as base as I.

"What I feel Princess, is that after years of aimlessness, the Lord has finally set a mission for me. The rapture which burst within me the day of our first meeting was not that of man for woman, but of man for God. Through you God has spoken to me, he has said Honour and serve this woman, for she is one of my greatest creations. Through this service shalt thou prove thy love for me.

"Princess, you are my portal to the Lord. You cannot deny me the honour of serving you, for to do so would be to deny me God."

When she returned to Tycho and I, Alexandra was speechless. She looked to me, as though I might have an argument for her, but I was as moved as she. Tycho looked into Alex's face, then mine, and seemed to grasp our thoughts. He stepped away, his bare hands tucked tightly under his arms. Bareheaded, the wind catching his sandy brown hair, Tycho stopped as Alex had at the nose of the Knight's horse.

The Knight and the storyteller formed an image which has forever been frozen into my memory. Tycho touched the horse's nose with his bare hand, looked sadly into its large brown eyes. Beauvais loomed silently above him, unmoving despite the chill wind, the flumes of snow, the ominous sound of tree branches brushing together in the winter silence.

When Tycho spoke he did not, at first, look towards Beauvais. Rather he kept his gaze fixed upon the horse's sad eyes. "Beauvais, what is it that you are dying for?"

The Knight paused a long while before answering, and I regretted again the steel visor hiding his face, hiding his emotions. "Storyteller, I'm so cold that I daren't move, and I believe that I will die upon this bridge, yet I know not why."

"Is it not for the Princess?"

"I came to this bridge for the Princess, and yet I do not feel my death is for her. It has another purpose, a true and worthy one, but I know not what it may be."

Tycho reached his cold hand again towards the horse's nose, rubbing his fingers through the star of white hair. "Beauvais, have you heard voices? Have you been bidden here by whisperings of the saints?"

"As La Pucelle? No. I envy her, envy her faith that the Lord spoke to her and so inspired her upon her mission. But I've heard only the shifting of ice below this bridge, the wind brushing the branches of trees together behind me."

"Then how can you be so certain that death here is your lot?"

"I am not certain."

"Yet you remain."

"Aye."

"You shall be dead by morning."

"Perhaps."

Tycho shook his head slightly, and with his back to me I could not see his face, yet the quiver in his voice made me think he was close to tears. "Beauvais, were your church to

194

judge, they'd claim I was corrupt indeed, but I shall pray for you; pray that death comes to you humbly, as a reward, not a punishment, to save you from this cold rather than inflict it upon you."

"I shall pray for you as well storyteller."

Tycho nodded but did not speak, looking for a short while at the Knight above him. He then bowed ever so slightly and turned, but halted as Beauvais said "Wait."

Beauvais loosed his fingers, and the lance he had held, one end stuck in the snow, fell from his hand. He moved this gloved hand to his horse's neck, and slowly, with much effort, raised his right leg behind him, across the shanks of his horse, and then he slid from his saddle down into the snow.

He shuffled awkwardly, saying quiet words to Tycho, who fetched a sword lying nearby, and placed it in the Knight's hands. Beauvais held the hilt before his chest, the blade end resting in the snow. "My horse, Tycho, you need to care for him. He must not share my death."

Tycho nodded. He took the horse's reins in his bare hands and coaxed him forward a few steps, finding the horse grateful for the movement. "Adieu, Beauvais," he said, turning his back to him, beginning to lead the horse away.

"Until God, storyteller," Beauvais replied.

Tycho led the horse from the bridge, the great animal stepping slowly through the snow. A few guards followed after the boy while the rest stayed with Alex and me. Alexandra stepped towards Beauvais, who was now standing rigidly in his silver armor in the middle of the bridge, snow up to his knees, trees waving in the grey distance behind him, his sword, blade into the ground, hilt before his breastplate, held before him.

Alexandra whispered, "Good luck, dear Knight." Beauvais replied "Merci Madame," and then Alexandra and I, with our guards trailing behind us, turned back towards the city.

Tycho had already reached the riverbank. He trudged strongly along the winding, snow covered road towards the walls and houses of the city. He held the horse's reins in his hands, the horse itself staying close beside him, seemingly grateful to have found a new master.

Beauvais died in the cold. His body was brought to the castle the day after we'd spoken to the Knight. "Merci Madame," were likely the last words he ever uttered.

TYCHO'S JOURNAL

APRIL 1431

The moonlight touched my bare arm. The night had settled around me. I was comfortable and at ease. When the hand stirred the waters of my sleep and brought pictures to life in my mind, I tossed, rolling onto my back, my eyelids flickering.

"Tycho," a voice whispered, stilling the waters again.

A woman was in the room. Her clothing was plain, a brown dress and white blouse, but rather conspicuously she wore a sword. She was neither young nor old, perhaps twenty, neither plain nor beautiful. The wonder was that she did not quite seem to fit within the room. An energy was within her, an energy which allowed me her name.

"Jeanne," I murmured.

La Pucelle smiled and nodded to me. She undid her sword belt and placed the long sword on my table, next to my Bible, which her fingers and her gaze danced over briefly. She climbed into bed with me. I lay on my back, the Maid on her side, her left arm bent, her head on her hand, her right hand upon my chest. "I need know your answer," she said.

A curious statement, but I knew her meaning. "Ahab's riddle?"

She nodded and I turned from her eyes to stare silently at the ceiling of my small room. The Maid's hand was a feather on my chest, but her presence was that of lying with an angel. "My answer," I whispered, "is Josef."

"Why?"

I closed my eyes. "Because no one should have to die alone."

La Pucelle ran her fingers lightly over my face, touching my lips and my closed eyes. Although it was almost imperceptible, I felt a brief touch of lips against my ear, and then the Maid curled her left arm into a pillow and lay still beside me. The night opened its arms again. I drifted away on the gentle waves of sleep.

1435

In the winter of 1431, I did not recognize the many currents which had begun to sweep through the castle. Save for Tycho's increasing silence and reclusiveness, I thought all was the same - Pawel continued in his midnight walks, another suitor had failed to win Alexandra's hand, Gora's curse, in the form of Agnieszka learning the truth of her imprisonment, was about to destroy another love story.

The change in Tycho was the only one of which I took note, for I thought that my young bouncing friend was becoming as spiritually broken as was I. He kept largely to himself, and due to his fear of the voices, he rarely slept. When we saw him he was ragged and exhausted, and most notably, he was silent.

I thought that it was Agnes who was giving him worry, but after reading his journal I realize that Tycho felt strangely content with the prospect of Agnes attempting an escape. Perhaps, on one of those cold nights he spent seated at his desk, reading or writing by candlelight, the story of Agnieszka and Michal was revealed to him in its entirety, and he knew that their story did not end with that goodbye near the lightning scarred tree.

If not Agnes, what troubled the boy?

He makes only brief mention of this in his journal, but I believe, especially in light of his speech concerning his wintry death, that he was afraid of travelling again. The boy, who had never known mother or father, whose closest friends had either died in Bohemia or abandoned him there, and who had never felt himself to be loved, was afraid of being alone.

When Tycho had accepted the post of court storyteller, he had renounced freedom for family, a trade he never regretted and would have ecstatically made again. In Gora, with Alexandra, Krysztoff, Agnieszka, Ahab and I about him, not to mention the scores of others at court who adored him, Tycho was the happiest he had ever been. He regaled listeners with stories of his adventures in foreign lands, making girls with dreamy eyes long to see the English white cliffs, the warren of caves and underground tunnels beneath Montsegur, the unbelievable expanse of blue ocean stretching from the Iberian coast, but Tycho did not wish to return to these places. He had experienced their beauty and mystery by himself, and preferred his home in Gora to the hard won delights of the road.

It was the prospect of losing his home and family which worried Tycho, which made him argue with Ahab when the astronomer raised the issue of the boy's destiny, and which made Tycho evade the midnight voices, voices which he felt would ask him to sacrifice the only thing he had ever valued, the only thing he wished to keep.

Although much was yet to happen, Tycho's entry regarding Jeanne d'Orleans was the last he made in his journal. It is Tonnelli who now steps from the shadows to take up the story, thankfully recording his thoughts and movements in his letters to Martin V, without which I would only sketchily have been able to draw this history to a close.

Tonnelli was soon to make a sacrifice as well, and I knew as little of it as I did the doubts which had visited Tycho. It is strange that I am the one who has become the historian - the blindest of the participants, and yet it is I who will engrave this story into history.

PART THREE

14

SPRING

THE MARKET

The fifth of May is a miserable day for dwarves. It is on this day that we celebrate the arrival of spring in Gora, and for decades now it has frustrated me terribly.

On the fifth of May young men bathe for the first time since autumn. They dress as finely as they are able, collect buckets which they fill with water, fetch elaborately carved sticks of wood, and then promenade into town to find women.

And the women are waiting. They stroll along the streets in whispering packs, eyeing the boys who lean against houses, sit on low walls, play dice with friends. If she fancies a boy, a girl will separate herself from her friends and move towards him, causing him to rise excitedly. The girl stops, smiles, and closes her eyes, while the boy lifts stick from bucket to send drops of water sparkling in flight towards the maid as a blessing upon her. She feels the wet touch on her cheek, opens her eyes as the boy mumbles a short prayer, hoping fervently that she will offer him a silent but unmistakable invitation to her affections.

Tycho delighted in the fifth of May. In spring 1430 he had almost caused a riot as the boys about him in Gora's market square watched in mounting rage as woman after woman had sauntered away from the storyteller, swaying her hips for his benefit, ignoring all the other boys in the market.

On May 5th, 1431, I awoke in a foul mood. The sky was blue and beautiful, girls were giggling, birds singing, and the scent of spring rose inspiringly through the air. A perfect day for the celebration, perfectly arranged to depress a dwarf who had never once been approached by a rosy cheeked girl. I stood for a short while in the castle courtyard where a small group of boys, amongst the swirl of animals and people, were sitting together, furiously whittling their sticks. As I stood watching them, Tycho emerged from a gateway.

He was running and passing the huddled whittlers he gaily called "Spring's here boys!" before disappearing within another gate. A moment later a young woman burst into the courtyard and wailed "Where's Tycho?" to the indifferent passers-by.

The boy was in a good humour again. That pleased me. For weeks he had been sullen and distracted, and it was good to see him responding to spring's call. Although I had resolved to avoid the market that day, I found myself curious about Tycho. I wanted to see if another riot was brewing, if Tycho was being chased through the streets, so in the early afternoon I made my way through the city to the market square. I skirted its crowded and bustling center, hugging close to the bordering buildings, and eventually spotted Tycho leaning against a low wall, three buckets of water at his feet. I rolled my eyes towards Heaven. The boy, apparently, had anticipated blessing every woman in the city.

Tycho was speaking to some lass as I approached. His arms were crossed across his chest, a brilliant smile upon his face. She leant forward, kissed Tycho on the cheek, moved away ever so slightly, touched her hand gingerly upon his crossed arms, seemed to reaffirm a promise of some sort, and then moved away, looking over her shoulder and waving just before she disappeared into the swirling crowd of people in the square.

Tycho watched her fade away and then looked about him. Seeing me he bounced my way, wrapped his arms about my waist and hoisted me into the air. "Samuel!" he cried, "Kiss Me!"

I spent the day with Tycho. I sat on the wall while the boy gave his blessings. I looked to our left and right where other boys sat at the market's edge, occasionally blessing girls who approached them, but often looking jealously towards my friend, and their jealousy was well founded. Young women simply flocked to Tycho. They appeared out of the crowd, their eyes focused intently upon him, and stood before the boy hinting, with every look and stirring of their bodies, that all they possessed was his for the asking.

Having long ago given up hope for love in my own life, I was able to watch Tycho in amusement rather than jealousy. But I left Tycho at one point to drink an ale in a pub, and while on my way across the square a young girl, who I'd not seen approach, stopped before me and said "Have you not water for blessings?"

I gaped at her for several seconds, and then, regretfully, said "No. I've not."

"Perhaps simply a blessing then."

She was in her middle teens, lacking charm of any sort, perhaps the plainest girl I had ever seen, yet she had spoken to me, and I was as dumbfounded as I'd have been if the Countess herself had beckoned me to her bed. I looked up into the girl's face and dug out of my soul a blessing I'd been preparing for sixteen years, a blessing of rainbows and sunrises and dreams such as only the Saints are sent.

She closed her eyes and curtsied when I finished, saying "Thank you kind sir." She vanished into the press of bodies in the market. I stood dazed for a short while, buffeted by the crowd, and then continued to the inn where I drank a reflective ale and found myself utterly incapable of preventing my thoughts from drifting around the girl who I'd blessed. My life's store of experience struggled desperately to convince me that I had vanished from her thoughts immediately after she'd turned away, yet still I dwelled upon her, thinking perhaps it could only be a girl as plain as she who would love a dwarf.

In the market, returning through the sunshine and crowds to Tycho, I spied the girl again. She was with the boy, standing before him, apparently having already received her blessing and now requesting other favours. As I came to his side she looked down upon me, bowed her head saying "Kind sir," then, smiling a final time for Tycho, she left us.

Tycho watched her disappear into the crowd while I trembled beside him, my arms hanging tautly at my sides, my hands clenched into fists. Tycho, not looking at me, pointed into the crowd and said "Agnieszka's coming," but I wasn't listening. In an impulse brought on by envy I picked up one of the buckets and threw all the water on Tycho, but, with my height, I succeeded only in drenching him below the waist.

Tycho smiled at me amusedly. He lifted a bucket and, very slowly, raised it above my head. I didn't move, only summoned my sourest look and muttered "Don't...", but Tycho tipped the bucket above my head. Water cascaded down onto me, spilling my hat onto the ground, matting my hair and soaking my clothes.

I remained still. The water had pasted my clothes to my skin, making me feel almost indecent as my leggings gripped my buttocks tightly. Finally I nodded, bit my lower lip, and narrowed my eyes, glowering at him. Tycho put his hands on his hips, bit his lower lip, and glowered back at me.

I burst out laughing.

Agnieszka had a basket hanging from her arm. She reminded us that the object of the day was for boys to sprinkle water upon girls, not to engage in water fights, and Tycho replied that she seemed strangely dry.

'I'm spoken for," she said. "I can't allow these lustful boys to be casting their wishes upon me."

Tycho lifted his right foot and began a series of light kicks, water flying about him.

"Agnes, it isn't necessary for you to sleep with everyone who sprinkles you with water."

"No, but I do believe that is what they hope for."

Tycho nodded, grinning. "Indeed. You're fortunate, are you not, that this little tradition doesn't fall in the summer? I would have chased you all about Gora last summer."

"I'd never have permitted you to sprinkle me with water, Tycho."

"Sprinkle!" Tycho exclaimed, shaking his other leg now. "Agnes, if waving a few drops of water onto a woman represents a boy's interest in her, last summer I'd have needed to flood you with bucket after bucket to represent the intensity of my desire."

Agnieszka smiled at him, the crowd a moving mass of bodies behind her. "Tycho, your fantasy world is so real for you, isn't it? I'd never have given you the opportunity to splash me with a bucket of water."

"Oh I don't know," Tycho said, and I knew immediately that Agnes had made a mistake. The boy bent and clasped the rope handle of his second bucket. "It isn't so arduous a task really."

The water shone in the sunlight as it flew towards Agnieszka. It landed upon her with the tinkling of a million little splashes. After the water hit there was a long, still silence. Agnes held her arms wide at her sides, her basket still hanging from her right forearm. She looked down at her dress, which was now clinging tightly to her body. When her reaction finally came it began as a vengeful and furious look cast at Tycho, the dropping of the basket, and a step taken with arms raised towards the boy. Tycho escaped her easily, laughing as he wove himself through her outstretched arms till he was beyond her, vanishing within the swirling crowd in the square.

I retrieved Agnieszka's basket and stood in the sunlight beside her, water running away through the crevices between the cobbled stones at our feet. She brushed at her dress, and then took long folds of it in her hands to wring it free of water. She sighed and stood up to her full height, reaching out her hand for her basket, which I handed her. "Ah Samuel," she said, "if I didn't love him so much I'd need to throttle him."

She looked so beautiful standing above me, the bell tower and the blue sky behind her.

"Yes," I said. "Yes I know the feeling. In fact I think I had the same feeling only moments before you arrived."

Agnieszka returned to the castle to change. I decided that the afternoon sun would dry me well enough and so stayed. The crowd was thinning somewhat, a few boys were tipping the water from their buckets and leaving. I looked about, enheartened by the fact that others had been as unsuccessful as I, and lost in this thought of shared misery, I almost failed to notice him. The Bishop stood perhaps thirty footsteps away. His arms hung limply at his sides. His mouth was open and I could see his chin damp with saliva. He seemed to be frozen.

TONNELLI

MAY 1431

Colonna:

I have written at times of revolution, of Christ returning to earth and purging of its sins the Church built in his name. The revolution may begin in Gora.

In the city market today, the boy storyteller cast a pail of water upon the cook Agnieszka, of whom I've written. As I write these words, hours later in my rooms, I continue to see her - her face wet and glistening with water, her features beautiful with shock, and then more beautiful still with rage. Her wet dress wrapped itself tightly about her body, revealing, in all their glory, her breasts and legs, firm and youthful.

I grow excited again, dear God.

I feel I am about to unloose a fire, and yet this conviction was born into me by an unbearable lust. What can be the nature of the fire I shall unleash? What sort of global change begins with a firing of the loins? And why is it I, who am as stricken with sin as a corpse is of worms, who shall broker this change?

My part in this drama is to reprise a customary role - the role I played before banishment to Gora, and concerns for my neck, caused me to abandon it. Even should it cost me my head, I can no longer suppress my lusts for Agnieszka. The sight of her today has caused everything within me to quiver. I shall approach her, tantalize her with words of the Lord, and bed her. I may even destroy her.

Odo, have you ever wondered, sitting upon your papal throne in Rome, choosing from a queue which prostitutes to allow entrance to your feasts, if evil is necessary? Why would the Lord create men such as we if this were not true? Perhaps peace and prosperity can only be appreciated if something must be overcome to achieve them. Perhaps the garden, before the snake lifted his head, was less a paradise than it was a place of stagnation. Can humanity evolve if it does not have a battle? Does the war against evil, or perceived evil, not give humanity a cause, and is the pursuit of a cause not the most glorious way to spend a life?

I feel Holy, possessed, as I finish this letter, by something divine. I've not felt this way since our time together in Velabro, when my sermons caused men to swarm the pulpit, reaching their arms towards me, believing I held the keys to Peter's gates.

I feel Holy, yet I prepare to seduce, possibly to rape. The revolution I sense, I wonder, shall it save me or damn me? Or shall I simply drop, as a stone into a lake, deep and forgotten beneath the surface of history?

Gieuseppi Tonnelli
Gora

THE STORY ROOM

The windows were thrown open, the smell of a spring evening drifted past. The Prince and Princess lay atop the bed, Agnieszka and I sat in our chairs, candles burnt in scattered groups throughout the room.

The boy was the last of us to arrive.

In recent weeks he had told us stories - a King declaring war on the sky, thinking that it had somehow killed his son, a Prince digging up the corpse of a long dead lover, placing her on the throne beside him, forcing all members of his court to kiss her corrupt lips - which had given us dark nightmares, made us nearly fear to see him enter the story room. But on this night, on this night, he said "Close your eyes," and just as I did, I saw that his eyes were bright, were smiling.

A boy loved a girl. He was fifteen years old, a jeweller's apprentice, and possessed of a voice which had never introduced itself to the world.

She was eighteen, daughter to the richest merchant in the city. She often visited the shop at which her admirer was employed, but spoke only to the master, oblivious to the young boy who stood in the shadows, drinking in the lilt of her voice, the fall of her hair, the orchestration of her movements. After each of her visits, as she rattled through the city in her father's carriage, she left behind, in that tiny shop, a heart pounding a hymn to her glory.

The boy was well aware of the obstacles before him. He was hardly more than an urchin, and she a child of the highest class. He was mute and she sparkling and gay. His master was a tyrant, and if informed of his apprentice's desires would likely imprison him in his dark back room. Yet the boy believed that love existed, that it existed for everyone, and in his silent world of tattered blankets and calloused hands he sought for a way to express his love, believing that if he were only able to accomplish this, she would discover a love for him as well.

As a jeweller the boy was a prodigy, yet this was known only to his master, who claimed credit for his apprentice's works, basking in the acclaim they garnered him. As the boy sought desperately for a way to reveal his love, he found himself unable to craft the jewelry which had been called the finest in northern Christendom. He lay in bed day upon day, subjected to fits and threats from his master, but these he hardly noticed, lost as he was in feverish dreams, in the dilemma of how to properly express love to one as fine as an angel.

He began, unconsciously at first, by simply remembering his dreams, which were always of the girl who had captured his heart. When he woke in the morning he lay staring at the ceiling, gathering and straightening his night's visions. He worked them with his mind as one would work a kinked and knotted rope by hand, working patiently to unravel the knots, ease away the kinks.

As time passed, as the dreams stockpiled, he began to feel them as a physical presence in his life. His fingers began to play upon them as though they were malleable as gold, and soon he found himself weaving a silken necklace of dreams, twisting them elegantly around each other like a rainbow of a million mingled colours.

He collected a box lined with velvet, placed within it his necklace of dreams, and stepped from his master's shop into the streets of snow. He struggled across the city and barely had he stopped in the street before her house then her door opened, and dressed for the winter cold she moved towards him.

She said "hello" in a friendly though questioning voice and he found himself circling the moment – detailing in his memory her frosty breath, red cheeks, wondrous green eyes. Finally he reached into his pocket and withdrew the small box. He removed from it a whisper of air, a shimmering of moonlight. He stepped close, stood upon tiptoe, and tenderly placed his creation about her neck.

She trembled. She closed her eyes as the force of his dreams flowed through her body; then she looked deeply into the eyes of the ragged boy before her. She smiled and said "Yes."

He remained still, staring up at the girl who seemed to him framed by a radiantly blue sky. He stared at the blush on her cheeks, at the puff of frosty air as she repeated the word again. "Yes."

Alexandra was staring at Tycho. He held her gaze a short while, then moved from the foot of the bed to its side, where he bent low over the Princess and kissed her forehead. He made a slow round of the bed, bending his face into Agnieszka's hair and kissing her head, kissing my cheek, and Krysztoff's, and then he left us.

As Alexandra noted that evening, it was his first story of a love which ended well.

TONNELLI

MAY 1431

Colonna:

The dinner hour passed, night began to fall, and I began a vigil outside the girl's door. I realize now that this was unwise, if she had returned in company my presence would have required an awkward explanation, and yet she returned alone. She had been with the Prince and Princess, listening to the boy's stories. I heard her footsteps sounding on the stones, growing steadily closer, then she turned into the short hall off of which lies her room, and where, in near darkness, I waited.

If she was surprised, she hid it well, for I must have appeared as a mountainous shadow rising above her. Barely able to see her face through the late evening shadows, we were silent. I was momentarily struck dumb - she was before me, standing proudly, strong, and yet barely visible in the darkness. Was it possible I dreamt?

"What do you want?"

All was real. I drew, from deep within, the quietly rumbling voice with which I was used to preach. "Agnieszka," I said. "We've not met. I am Bishop Tonnelli."

"I know," she answered, a wariness in her voice which I would have to soothe. "I know. I am Agnieszka."

"Yes, you are." I lifted a hand in the darkness, motioned towards her closed door. "Shall we enter? The Lord has destined that our paths are to cross. I have words for you."

She was still. She did not sway nor did the glow of her face flicker in movement. I feared that I had failed before truly beginning. Then the phantom before me spun slowly as though performing a macabre dance. She pushed open her door and said "please."

In her room, as she moved about setting candles to life, I struggled to control my nerve. Fire in her hand, her shadow looming on all the walls, she was swelling in my imagination from a girl over whom I lusted, to an enchantress. I expected her momentarily to turn on me, lay open every sin I'd ever committed and feast upon them, and then upon me. For moments that lingered too long I saw her as a vampiress, bending naked and bent and cold into my essence. I saw an evil rippling laugh roil across her face, her tongue lustily lick through my soul, and like hot grease, I saw my soul spill from her mouth and over her lips, dripping grossly from her chin.

But no. She sat upon a chair. She clasped her hands in her lap. She gazed patiently up at me. She was human only. She was human. I turned away to find my breath, to organize the words. "My dear," I said, looking not at her, but at the shuttered window, "are you ever alone?"

I had turned my back to her, she was behind me, and the thought of her as a vampiress rose again, shivering a chill into my spine. Then her voice, meek and soft, breathed "Yes" into the stillness of the room.

I was fearful of facing her, lest the torment of my thoughts become apparent, but slowly I turned - the candles, the shadows, then the girl, erect and poised in the center of the room. "Have you ever turned to the Lord in times of loneliness, Agnieszka?"

She dropped her eyes, and I took what seemed my first breath since entering the room. She spoke quietly for a short time, almost apologetically explaining her beliefs, which did not include a being whose celebrated benignity was seldom evident in a land where every day brought a new challenge to survival. Her thoughts brought no surprise, I'd heard similar foolishness often in this unholy land. The predictability of her words comforted me.

She was a young girl; no different from others I'd performed this scene with in years previous. With familiarity I was granted control, and when her timid speech was finished, when she raised her eyes from their focus on the floor, I sat in a chair across from her.

"Yes," I said softly, my voice dripping with tenderness. "Yes." And then, with a well-practiced logic, and well-acted emotions, I gave her a brief introduction to God's love.

She has promised to meet me again.

Gieuseppi Tonnelli
Gora

TONNELLI

MAY 1431

Colonna:

It happened that I was dreaming of her when she knocked upon the door. The Lord it would seem is fond of coincidence. At the insistence of the raps I came descending lightly from my fantasies. My mind clear I rose and answered the caller. She was standing on my step, the street dark and silent behind her. Verily she was the incarnation of the dreams from which I'd just awoken, and perhaps it was at this moment, at this conjunction of dream and reality that I rendered all that was to follow inevitable.

I motioned for the girl to enter. I stood to the side, but with my girth, in that narrow doorway, her arm swept across my belly, her skirts brushed my legs. She passed me and entered within my rooms. I stood, for long moments, looking out at the night. The slight touch of her arm, of her clothing, and I was adrift. My hands shook, my face twitched. I attempted to breathe deeply, to discover my composure, but it would not come. The girl was waiting for me. I closed the door more slowly than my reluctant soul shall enter Hell, and I turned.

In my study there burned a fire. She stood in the center of the room, light and shadows rippling on the walls about her. I paused. I wondered if still I were dreaming, if the rapping I had heard had been deception, if this was dream masquerading as reality. To the vision before me I spoke. "Girl," I said, "speak truly, are we now but shades?"

The girl was confused. A shade would have answered cunningly. All was real. I motioned, and with a shush of cloth, a creaking of wood, we sat.

Once upon a time, before my banishment to Gora, I felt at this moment as though my spirit left my body. The quiet firelit room, the words I employed, looks I cast, even my gestures, were all so natural, so well rehearsed, that I was able to seduce my prey as though by instinct. I drifted away. I rose up in spirit and hung about the ceiling, looking down to see my physical self enact the scene of hypnotic seduction.

But that was long ago. On this night, with this girl, the hypnosis was not successful. She fought even as I spoke, and I realized, perhaps before even beginning, that I had betrayed myself.

She may have seen my hands shake as I'd closed the door. She may have seen a glint of fear in my eyes. Perhaps she has the power of inner sight and viewed plainly my soul. I know not what alerted her, but the girl fought me. I found my words encountering the wall of her mistrust. Recognizing the wall I sought for more passion, more eloquence, but it became a farce. The more desperately I sought for control the more thoroughly I perceived that she was growing amused. Agnieszka's silence in the face of my verbosity was winning the evening. I grew weaker. The fire passed from me. I began to mumble rather than preach. I insisted that I was her saviour, but she had seen the devil behind my eyes. I stopped.

She had not spoken since entering my rooms, and she did not speak now. We sat facing each other. The fire crackled at our side. I felt her to be mocking me with her silence, and an anger rose within me. "This changes little," I hissed.

Her eyes narrowed slightly. "Sir?"

"I have little time left, little time to enjoy the bounty of the earth. Do not underestimate the measures I will stoop to use."

She did not respond, in words. Rather she rose and attempted to leave, but I reached forward clutching her wrist, my great fingers holding her still. "Agnieszka... "

"Tonnelli, a word from me to the Prince and Princess and your head shall drop into the basket at daybreak."

"Agnieszka... "

"Control your lusts, only a short while is left, for if I am your only temptation I shall be gone soon enough."

"Gone? Where do you go?"

"My contract is nearly finished. Come June I will have been in Gora a year. I am returning home."

I stared at the girl for several moments, my hand still clutching her wrist as she stood high beside me. As it dawned on me that she was serious, that she truly believed herself to be returning home, I released my clutch upon her, eased back into my chair. "Good God, girl," I whispered. "Do you not realize the situation you are in?"

A sweep of doubt crossed her face, and in her bewilderment lay my answer. "Agnieszka, whatever this contract of yours stipulated is worthless. Where the children are concerned there are no contracts, save the unwritten one which is locked in the trap of Pawel's mind."

"What...?"

"You must have heard of Sam's old partner, and the storyteller who preceded Tycho?"

"They left."

"Left! My God, girl! They were murdered!"

She backed away from me as though I was the devil, and perhaps for the next few moments I was. I strode against her, pushing her against the wall with my great bulk, pinning her face before me. "Agnieszka, they were killed because they wanted to leave Gora. That is the unwritten contract. If you make the children happy then you are here for life. If you try to escape you are killed, and if you neglect your duties in an attempt to be dismissed, you are also killed. Why do you think Ahab and the dwarf and the storyteller are still here? Pawel won't allow them to leave."

I began then to nuzzle upon her neck, my lips and great tongue coursing in waves from shoulder to ear, and for several long moments, too bewildered by my words to worry about my actions, she allowed me licence.

So close to rapture, so close to creating in reality my nighttime fantasies, I moaned as I ran my hand against her breast, and in the shudder of arousal I relaxed, for merely a moment, but in that moment she found the freedom to move a leg. A knee struck me heavily in the place of my excitement. I slumped slightly, and with her feet upon the wall rather than the floor she pushed forward, sending me falling from her.

She flew from my rooms.

Odo, she may be on her way to Pawel. I should be alarmed, yet rather I feel oddly divine, strangely at ease.

And still vividly aroused. I wonder if this is how I shall meet death.

Gieuseppi Tonnelli
Gora

AGNIESZKA AND PAWEL

As Tycho and I drank in the kitchen, the great room black save for the effort of two candles we'd placed on our table, Agnieszka burst upon us like a wild animal, tumbling chairs from her path as she raced through the midnight room. Too frightened to be surprised that it was the Bishop who'd told her the truth, we confirmed what he'd said, and Agnes, a demented fury upon her face, shouted "THAT BASTARD" and hurtled back towards the entrance. Suddenly sober, Tycho and I exchanged a quick look and scampered off in pursuit of her.

We both knew her intention - in her fury she would find Pawel and scream amends from him, and we knew that this couldn't happen. Pawel, confronted by a hysterical woman screaming curses and insults at him, might simply kill her, and so we caught up with Agnes and pulled at her arms, but she was stronger than us both, and she kept shaking free, cursing us the whole time.

I fear I am painting this scene comically, despite its severity. This should give me worry, but it doesn't, for it is comic now, thinking back. Agnes hadn't a clue where to find Pawel, and after a year in Gora she still barely knew her way around the castle. Tycho and I, the boy vowing as he ran that all would be well, that he would escape with her, chased Agnes, who was barreling along like a mad boar, through the labyrinth halls of the castle, flinging my friend and me against the walls for our concern.

Finally, coming to another crossing of pitch-black halls, Agnes stopped, looked down the three routes available to her, and screamed "Bloody Hell! Where are we?"

Tycho and I approached her warily, stopping well out of her arm's reach. "Agnes," I said, "I can bring you to Pawel and yet you must promise me one thing before we depart."

She was upon me in instant, grabbing handfuls of my sweater and hoisting me into the air. "I'll promise nothing Samuel," she hissed. "Where is he?"

I was petrified, but I like to imagine that I exhibited a touch of courage that night. "You'll promise me this one thing," I replied, quaking, "or we won't go."

"What?"

"You must merely watch him, for a short while, in utter silence, before approaching him."

She was only a tall bristling shadow before me, so dark were the halls, but I saw the shadow give assent. "Aye," she said softly, lowering me.

Our long chase through the castle had shown me that Pawel was not following Kristina this night, and so there were only two other places to search for the King. I led my friends through the silence of the castle towards the story room, and then past it, to the wing where the children's' rooms were located. I pressed my ear to one door, listened, and then moved along the hall to another door, listening here as well. I stood back and turned to my friends. "He's within."

Agnes looked about her. "This is Krysztoff's room."

"Aye."

"How do you know he's within?"

I was already leading them down the hall. "For there are two people breathing in that room, and the King's breaths are like none other on this earth."

Next to Krysztoff's bedroom there is a small chamber used for storing linens and furs and pillows. I pushed the door open, entered, and unlocked the shutters upon the window, admitting a swath of moonlight into the room. Agnes and

Tycho watched silently as I pushed a chair next to the wall, then placed a small crate upon the chair. Clambering up onto my improvised ladder I quietly removed a stone from the wall and peered through the gap.

I stepped down and removed the crate. I touched Agnes's hand and guided her to the chair. She stepped up and pressed her face to the small opening.

She saw a long, richly furnished room, lit by only two or three candles. She saw a canopied bed in which lay a sleeping form, and near the bed, seated motionlessly upon a chair, she saw Pawel of Gora.

In a whisper, she asked what was occurring, and I replied that there was no mystery, that he was simply watching his son, as on other nights he watched his daughter. He guarded their sleep, happy enough if Kristina came to observe them, but unwilling to allow other ghosts or spirits to visit his children.

Agnieszka stepped down into Tycho's supporting arms. She stood quietly, gazing towards the floor, and then her eyes moved to Tycho's. "Will you truly run with me?"

"Yes."

She nodded. "When?"

AGNIESZKA AND TYCHO

Over the next few weeks I felt as though a secret plotter in some uprising. We met late at night in Tycho's room, discussing and discarding plans for my friends' escape. Then one night Agnes shocked the boy and I by announcing that all was well, that an escape route had been provided.

"Provided?" I repeated. "By whom?"

"The Bishop."

She had visited him to see if he could be controlled by his lusts. She pretended to have much lost her wit, to be distraught, in need of comfort. Tonnelli met her with kindness, but his every word requested more. Agnieszka promised herself to him, but demanded that the act itself must occur beyond the Barbican wall. It would utterly shatter her, she said, to need pass, for the rest of her life, the spot where she had been unfaithful to her husband.

Tonnelli should have sensed the danger, the duplicitousness, within this proposal, but he had agreed to find for them a route through the Barbican. He conferred several days with some of the less lustrous denizens of the city, and then met again with Agnes. He told her of a tavern in the old city, named after its proprietor Obara, which did not quite rest against the Barbican wall. Between the wall and the tavern ran a narrow twisting alley, and carefully hidden in the shadows behind Obara's was a concealed passage through the Barbican wall.

Tonnelli proposed that they meet in the shadows behind Obara's tavern, walk through the passage together, and once in the outer city retire to the house of a friend. Agnieszka agreed, adding that on the night in question she would deliver to him a wondrous meal, a meal she would cook herself, and which would prime him for the pleasures of the evening.

"But Agnes, if Tonnelli sees you and I together he will know that he is being deceived, that we are planning to flee."

"He will not see us."

"But Agnes..."

"He will not see us for he shall not meet us in that alley behind Obara's tavern. The meal I deliver him will be the last of his life. It will be wondrous indeed, but lethal as well. I shall poison him, he will die in his rooms, and you and I, Tycho, will use his escape route ourselves."

Tycho and I stared at Agnieszka for a long while. The aspect of her face seemed to alter in the candlelight. She seemed, illuminated spectrally in the greater darkness of the room, some manner of phantom. "Agnieszka, truly, can you kill him?"

Her gaze met mine. "Samuel, if I could guess a dosage which would merely make him sleep I would be more merciful. But with his size... Samuel, if he staggers to the tavern, if he sees Tycho and I and raises the alarm, if he simply causes midnight eyes to turn in that direction, we are lost."

"But, to take a life... "

"Samuel, Tonnelli threatened me with rape. I would normally concur that simply threatening a crime should not deserve death, but I do not feel charitable at this time. A year of my life, the first year of my marriage, has been stolen from me. If I must murder a detestable rapist to return home, so be it. I will be able to live with that upon my conscience."

She stared long at me, a hard determined look, almost warning me not to disagree. The idea of Tonnelli's death disturbed me, but I did not raise my voice, did not ask how she had been made able to judge innocence. I leaned back from the small table and turned my eyes to Tycho, who was looking neither at Agnes nor I. He was staring out the open window, contemplating the distant swath of starry sky.

15

MAY 31, 1431

EVENING

I sat quietly on a stool, my hands clasped, my elbows resting upon one of the kitchen's immense wooden tables. Late afternoon sunlight shone through the windows, people moved about preparing dinners, several different conversations hung in the air. This was a scene I had witnessed a thousand times. A scene of quiet beauty, of comfort, yet a chill of fear lay within me.

Agnieszka had already prepared the Prince and Princess's meals. They had been set atop a hearth to keep warm. She was now preparing a third meal. Knives flashed, ladles dipped and emptied, spices set cunningly adrift in the air, and then something not quite so normal occurred. Agnes reached her hand into a pile of cloths. A tiny bottle flashed in her hand, was uncorked and tipped above the food before her, then disappeared again into the cloths. She did not look up nor pause, and in the room about us pinching hands continued to be slapped away, exclamations muttered, cutlery dropped. No one in that busy kitchen had perceived anything amiss, yet Agnieszka's fingers were now playing with death.

She exhaled a long breath, stepped back, and took up a rag with which to wipe her hands. She brushed a bang of hair from her eyes and looked softly towards me. A single word, mouthed but not spoken. "Finished."

Tycho was late that night in coming to the story room. Agnieszka did not appear at all. When I arrived Alexandra had tried to speak with me, but I was distracted. I leant against the wall by the window and looked out at the dark fields, the stars, the bright silvery moon.

When Tycho entered he seemed surprised to see me, standing still and staring my way for several moments. I threw another log upon the fire then sat down in a chair near the bed. Tycho assumed my position by the window, staring off into space.

Alexandra glanced from me to the boy, both of us silent and lost. "I sense something is amiss," she said.

Tycho turned from the window. Our eyes met briefly, and I let the storyteller tell the lie. He coughed slightly and said "Aye. I feel a sickness tonight Princess."

Alexandra threw back the covers and moved from the bed. Without slipping her feet into her shoes she crossed the cold floor to stand beside Tycho. She raised her arm and pressed her hand against Tycho's forehead. Tycho closed his eyes.

The Princess held her hand to Tycho's brow for a long time, finally whispering "You've no fever." She lowered her hand to place her palm flat against the boy's chest, as though here to find his illness. She was about to speak but Tycho placed a gentle finger against her lips. He raised his other hand to her shoulder and turned her back towards the bed, where she again settled herself under the covers. Tycho shook Krysztoff's shoulder. The Prince groggily opened his eyes and muttered "What?"

"Come young one," Tycho murmured. "You must be awake tonight."

"I'll not tell you a story this evening," Tycho said, leaning forward in Agnieszka's chair. "Rather something about myself, about my past.

"When I was young, I travelled the length and breadth of Christendom. I seldom remained in one village for over a fortnight, and though it be a dubious honour, I may hold the distinction of having stolen chickens in more Kingdoms than any man alive.

"Though I have no place to call home, I know not where I was born nor do I have any recollection of siblings or parents, I did have one long settled period in my life. I lived for four years in Bohemia with a group who supported a churchman named Jan Huss. The years I spent in Bohemia were ones of war, as we fought both the Holy Roman Empire and forces recruited by the Pope.

"The group amongst whom I lived have been named the Hussites, and they had two different leaders during my time with them. The first was Zizka, whose name means One Eye, for he had, in battle, lost use of one of his eyes. The second was Procopius, who gave me the Bible I am used to read. I respected and admired Procopius, but of the two, my friend was Zizka.

"But friend is not the correct word. Zizka took pride in me, he made things possible for me. He ensured that I was comfortable and fed, and after every battle he sent a runner to find me and vouch that I was safe. I've little personal experience with this word, yet I'll say that Zizka was a father to me."

Tycho rose and wrapped his arms across his chest, moving from the bed to the fire. He watched it dance for a short while, and then turned his back to it, moving towards us across the dark room, his eyes upon the floor, softly kicking at the scattered wooden toys. "Zizka once took me with a small scouting party he was leading to check a dubious report that a small group of Papal soldiers were camped near us. We rode out in the early morning, the sky above a mass of dark and angry clouds. We found the bend in the river where the Guelphs were purported to be, found a family of surprised and wandering gypsies, shared some stories and a rabbit with them, and then we turned and headed back.

"It was a complete waste of our time, and as we rode some of the soldiers grumbled and cursed, especially because the clouds above were so black it seemed almost night, though at most it was mid afternoon. The sky burst when we were halfway through an immense field, rain pummeling us so heavily it felt like God was trying to hammer us into the ground.

"I must have had a terribly sour and miserable expression upon my face, because Zizka turned in his saddle, looked at me, and began laughing so heartily that he tumbled from his horse. I sat, and the soldiers sat, our reins in our hands, shoulders hunched, water running in rivers from our horse's necks, while our leader rolled in the grass laughing like a child told the finest joke in all creation.

"Finally he quieted. I dismounted and helped him rise, and, strangely, we did not remount. We took our horses' reins in our hands and began walking them through that rain soaked field, heading slowly towards the forest where we could gain shelter. Zizka put his hand on my shoulder and said It's just one day, Tycho. I looked up at him, saw the smile in his eyes, his comfort with life and its trials, and the rain and hunger and saddle sores vanished from my mind. Zizka had suddenly made everything well."

Tycho was wandering back and forth through the darkness, occasionally displacing toys with his feet. He spoke softly and almost to himself, and then he stopped pacing and stood at the end of the bed, catching my eyes, and then the Prince and Princess's. "We took Prague in 1424, and I lost Zizka in 1424. He died of the plague. I was twelve years old.

"I was quite bitter for a long while. I hardened my heart to others and eventually retook the road, alone, for fear of again losing someone. But life is difficult to deny, difficult to remain apart from. I told you of Zizka because I wanted to tell you something true tonight, something of consequence in my life. I've not battled dragons or rescued maidens, but I've lost a friend, a father, and survived..."

He had more to say, but I saw that he had lost the thread. He stared at Alex and Krysz from the foot of the bed, and then stepped onto the bed itself. He lowered himself on his knees between the outstretched legs of the children, and kissed each of them upon the cheek. "All will be well," he said, his voice hushed.

These were his last words to them.

TONNELLI

MAY 1431

Colonna:

I do not believe that I shall write again. As with all else, six years of letters, of venting my rage and describing my amusement, tonight comes to a close.

I am saddened by this. I once thought of you as my confessor, and then, with the passage of years, the evolution of my thoughts, my letters became virulent attacks against the church. Perhaps I raged against my own sin, and I wonder if this process was a cleansing one - if I am more pure, through the benefices of my letters, than I was six years ago when you first banished me to Gora.

If this be the case I have you to thank, and it is ironic, for you never read my letters. The most Christian act of your career, freeing a man from his sin, and you will be unaware of performing it.

With what am I left on this night? I have neither friends nor family and save for my small flock, I am a non-entity in the city which has been my home for six years. What plagues me most greatly this night, the burden beside which isolation is merely a moment's prick, is the knowledge that I have never returned to the world the love and kindness I took from it with the rapes and beatings of my youth.

Forgiveness is a great Christian belief, but if Hell exists, it must exist for me. I have committed crimes which must have caused much delight in the underworld, demons drooling in anticipation of taking hold of my soul, and so I will make a wish tonight, in this my last letter. I do not expect to escape punishment, I am prepared for my eternity of damnation, but

I should like to meet the true Christ - the Christ who kicked over the tax collector's tables, not the one our priests invoke when collecting their mortuaries. I should like to meet the true Christ, the man who said, "love thy neighbour," the man who wanted us to be kind to each other, the man who was worth a church even were he not the son of God.

Perhaps Odo, if only for a moment, and merely to wish me peace, He will visit me in Hell.

Odo, my wish for you, is that you one day find the true Christ, and turn your Church towards him – towards kindness, Odo. For surely, and for all of us, it is needed.

Gieuseppi Tonnelli
Gora

THE WELL

I found Agnieszka lying upon her bed, a candle burning on her table. She was silent and I took this to mean she was frightened. I whispered her name causing her to stir and sit up. She swung her legs to the floor and wrapped her arms around me. I stood warm in her embrace for an age, and then led her to the door, into the hall, through the castle, into the courtyard. The stars bright and the moon full above us, Agnes whispered "It is a clear night. It is a good sign, is it not?"

"Yes," I lied. The moon shone as the sun, it dazzled my eyes and sent our shadows shimmering onto the ground. A boy and a girl walking on a night like this, they would be visible for leagues. Better it was raining, I thought. Better the clouds hung low and sent sheets of dark water about you, hiding you as though behind veils. I squeezed her hand tightly in mine and smiled up into her eyes. "Yes," I said. "It is a beautiful night."

We passed through the first gate and began our descent through the crooked and cobbled streets of the inner city. The ramshackle buildings loomed over us, lights glimmered through windows. Sometimes, distantly, we could hear shouting and laughter spilling into the night from a tavern. The farther we walked the more Agnes clung to me, and I found her fear to be infectious. My mouth dried and my voice was stilled. I clung to Agnes, feeling the frightened child within one of Tycho's midnight fairy tales.

We were descending a street which led into the market square, which we had to cross to reach the web of streets where Obara's tavern sat, when we heard voices calling out before us. We paused to listen, and as the voices swelled and excitement grew we heard footsteps, the sound of someone running.

Around a corner and only a whisper in the darkness, Tycho came flying up the street. He barely stopped but rather swept us into his arms, turned us about and had us speeding away with him. "Agnes!" he gasped. "The Bishop's not dead!"

I tried to pull him to a stop, shouting his name and tugging his arm. "Wait! Tycho what did you see? Did Tonnelli see you?"

"Aye," Tycho answered, continuing to pull me along with him. "He's lying in the street in front of the tavern, vomiting like a demon, yelling Agnieszka's name, and when he spotted me he began yelling my name, and TREACHERY! The plan is shattered, Samuel."

My mind raced. Tycho and Agnes had to escape this night. If Pawel suspected anything he would, at the very least, begin to guard them bodily, preventing them from gaining the chance again. As the shouts rose behind us, as lights fired in the buildings around us, I squeezed Tycho's hand and shot in front of him.

I led them back to the castle. When we turned that final corner and the defensive wall about the castle loomed before us Tycho shouted my name questioningly but I paid him no heed. We raced through the gate and into the courtyard. I pulled them into the shadows against the castle wall and we snuck into the northwest corner, where sat the only well in the castle.

Tycho put his hands on the low wall and looked into the darkness within. "A drink would be Heaven," he gasped. "Good idea, Sam. We'll run for our lives after we've had a bit of a rest."

"Quiet fool," I said. "You know the story don't you?"

"What story?"

"Of Prince Gora, after whom this land is named."

Tycho shook his head, his shoulders rising and falling with his deep breaths.

"The most famous story in Gora," I began, "is of how a young Prince, 400 years ago, killed a dragon that lived in the caves which stretch below the castle and have their exit in the cliffs that overlook the river south of the city. The dragon ate livestock and children and was impossible to kill for when he was outside he was either in flight, or swimming mightily through the river, and when he was at rest he lay within his cave, protecting its entrance with his fiery breath.

"400 years ago it was believed that the water which lay within this well led to pools within the dragon's cave. Prince Gora filled a cow's intestines with sulphur, and then covered the sulphur with a sheepskin. He had himself lowered into this well, and touching the water he dove and swam, and swam, eventually surfacing in a deep blackness. He swam until his feet touched ground, and carrying the sheepskin of sulphur he walked out of the pool and into a maze of stony passages.

"The Prince was fortunate in that there were no forks in the passage, no decisions to be made regarding direction. After he'd gone a long way he began to hear a rumbling snore echoing towards him. He kept walking and his narrow passage emptied into a great cavern, in which lay an immense shadow which the Prince recognized to be the dragon.

"The Prince positioned himself before the dragon and both shouted and tossed the bundle of sheepskin at the same moment. The dragon's eyes flashed open to see something hurtling towards him. He opened his mouth to swallow it, and landing within the fiery furnace which was his stomach was a ball of sulphur which ignited and caused an eruption within. Fire, more than he could survive, burst from the dragon's nostrils and mouth and ears. He soared out of the cave, fire blazing about him, and dove into the river, where he drank and drank attempting to extinguish the flames within him. He was successful in extinguishing the flames and yet he drank so much water that he swelled to twice his normal size, and staggering on the riverbank he exploded - his death marked by an explosion of fireworks in the night sky."

When I finished, I stood looking questioningly into Tycho's face, but then Agnieszka gripped my shoulders, blurting "Stories! Samuel we're about to die here!"

"Agnes, Agnes," Tycho interrupted, putting his hands on her shoulders. "What Samuel has told us is a legend which, if we are willing to trust it, will provide our escape."

She stared at him. "Are you saying you want to jump into this well?"

"I'll jump into anything with you anytime," he smiled, unable to resist a quick joke. "But yes, our escape must be now Agnes, and this appears to be the only way."

Agnieszka stepped into Tycho and put her hands on his cheeks, reading his eyes deeply. She then shifted her hands onto his shoulders and touched her forehead to his chest. Tycho kissed her on the top of her head and the cries and shouts which had, for the time of my story, been faint and distant, began to sound just outside the castle gate. "So be it," Agnieszka sighed.

Tycho pulled a knife out of a long bag which I only now saw hanging across his body. "When you've lowered Agnes down," he said, "cut the rope, tie my knife to one end and lower it to me. We shall need both rope and knife tonight." I nodded and began to mutter a few words of goodbye, but Tycho shook his head. "No," he said. "My goodbyes are in your room already Sam, and I've not the heart to hear yours."

He stepped up onto the waist high wall about the well and grasped the rope which hung from a beam, a bucket at its end. Agnes and I took hold of our end and braced our feet. Tycho stepped off the wall and dropped into the darkness. Moments later a splash marked his arrival at the bottom.

Agnieszka kissed me three times, twice for luck and once for the future. I lowered her into the darkness. I cut the rope and tied it about the knife. Following its clatter down the wall, Tycho took the knife safely and the rope was pulled from my hands.

I listened as Tycho whispered instructions to Agnieszka, their voices rising as though from the center of the earth. My name was called, I answered, and Tycho said "Adieu."

My friends were gone.

EPILOGUE

EPILOGUE

The year is now 1435.

B ishop Tonnelli, with Agnieszka's poison coursing through his veins, died the day following their escape. I heard of his death while confined in my room, and using Ahab as my agent, I pushed for his rooms to be searched. The letters which were found were given to Ahab, who held them for me until I was released.

Pawel died in 1433. Those of us who knew well of the King's demons were relieved. Since 1417 Pawel's life had been one of pain and regret, and I attended his funeral almost joyfully, thinking that he could now rejoin Kristina and find in the afterlife the happiness which he had known for only five short years on earth.

Krysztoff succeeded his father, and the first act of his reign was to find Agnieszka. He sent scouts to the lands all about Gora and she was eventually found in a small village near Gdansk. She was told that the new King of Gora, whose meals she had cooked and whose hair she had brushed, would be honoured if she would consent to return, with her entire family, to the city from which she'd once escaped.

She accepted.

I waited for my friend on the bridge over the Ardo river. It was summer; the sun beat down on my shoulders and shone like dazzling gems on the surface of the water. The road which led to the bridge came through a forest, and after waiting an entire morning, the forest opened to reveal a group of horse and riders, arrayed both before and behind a large carriage. The caravan approached the river slowly. The first riders climbed onto the bridge, near the spot where Beauvais had once stood. The wheels of the carriage began to clatter over the stones, and then one of the carriage doors burst open.

Agnieszka's long brown hair flew about her shoulders. The joy on her face made me tremble, and I stood breathlessly as she wove through the horses before her and ran to me, shouting my name into the sunshine. She caught me up in her arms and held me so close that for several moments my feet dangled in the air.

"SAMUEL!" she cried, her hands on my shoulders, holding me at arm's length. "Samuel!" her face radiant, beaming at me. "You'll want to know the story."

MAY 31, 1431

Kicking his legs to keep himself afloat in the dark water of the well, Tycho tied one end of the rope about his waist. The other end he placed in Agnieszka's hand to enable her to follow him as they swam through the black water. They dove and swam, and swam.

Underwater, in utter darkness, in a confined space, her lungs ready to burst, Agnes began to feel a rise of panic. Then she felt the rope in her hand angle suddenly upward. Close behind Tycho she burst above water into a darkness as complete as that below. They felt about with their hands and found that only in one place was their pool of water not bound by steep walls. They swam until their feet touched rock, and then they walked out of the pool, their voices scurrying away from them down invisible tunnels.

Still holding the rope, Agnes followed as Tycho led her down a narrow passage. The echo of their footsteps rose eerily around them, and gradually, as they moved further, their footsteps resonated differently. Feeling about the walls, listening to the echo of their voices, they realized that they were in an immense cavern. They continued to walk, hugging close to one wall, wary of the vast open space which they sensed on their left. As they moved they disturbed objects on the ground, objects which rattled and clinked like coins or rusting armor, and yet, in the unbroken darkness, were unidentifiable.

After skirting the edge of the cavern for a long while they came to another passageway. Tycho again led the way and Agnieszka followed him, the rope in her hand, ducking her head due to the gradually lowering roof. Then she bumped solidly into the boy. Wondering why he had halted, she whispered "What is it?" The words ricocheted behind her down the stony passage. "Your feet, Agnes," Tycho answered.

They stood ankle deep in water. Agnieszka feared that they had walked a circle in the cavern, returning to the pool from which they'd come. Tycho found her arms and stilled her, then removed the rope from her grasp. "Wait," he whispered. "Don't stir a foot. I shall be back."

The boy waded into the water and told her again not to move. The slightest of splashes and he was gone. Agnes whispered his name into the darkness but there was no answer. She wrapped her wet arms about her and closed her eyes, listening to the water lap at her feet, her nervous breath whispering off the walls about her.

After an eternity Tycho burst from the water, shouting her name, frightening her so badly she toppled backwards. But his next words thrilled her. "I found the river Agnes! I saw the stars!" She stepped into the water and Tycho pressed the rope into her hand. They dove, and passing through a confusion of currents which seemed to buffet her from all sides, she sensed that they had entered a much different body of water. Tycho had arched above her now, and following him she saw the water grow minutely lighter, and then shimmering specks appeared. She broke the surface, gasping, almost crying at the sight of stars and moon.

Tycho was beside her, his hair matted to his head, a smile bright on his face. They were bobbing in the middle of the river, the lights and dark mass of Gora visible down the river on their right. "Come Agnes," the boy whispered. "Move quietly. Sound travels far tonight, and the moon above illuminates us as though it were the sun."

They swam to what Agnes considered the wrong riverbank. "Tycho," she whispered, "this is the city side of the river."

"Aye, for I have to return a moment to the city."

She yelled "WHAT?!" so loudly it made dogs bark and caused them both to dive to their bellies and lie in the mud and grass of the bank for long anxious moments.

"Agnes," Tycho explained, "on foot from the very outset our chances are nil. We have to get away from Gora and into the countryside as fast as we can. We need a horse."

"But what if you're caught?"

"If I can't return I'll at least lead them astray. I'll cause a festival of noise in the city and hearing it you must go. Sneak into the forest, run like a wolf through the trees, and come daylight bury yourself deep into the best hiding place you can find. Keep careful note of where the sun sets every night, run in the direction of the sunset. Trust no one for at least five days and then choose the kindest person you come across and ask them how to find Kozle."

Tycho instructed Agnes to swim across the river and wait for him at the other end of the bridge. They parted, she entering the river and he running low along the bank towards the city. Having crossed the river Agnieszka pulled herself up into a hollow where the bridge met land. It was the beginning of summer and yet, in the night, sitting in sodden clothes, she shivered.

A breeze swept through the leaves of the forest behind her, creating a sound of constant whispering. The bridge was close enough to the city that she could hear voices, distant but audible - the cries and calls of soldiers organizing to pursue her. She clutched her arms about her, listening to the night's hundred sounds, and then she heard the rain.

The sound was of a tiny but terrible storm approaching the river from the city. The disturbance grew louder and louder and then exploded onto the distant end of the bridge. Finally, as the sound echoed over the river, Agnieszka realized that it wasn't rain, but rather the hooves of a horse, a horse in full flight, mercilessly pounding the ground.

The clamour of hooves on stone crossed the river and stopped above her. Agnes heard Tycho call her name. She came out from beneath the bridge and saw, in the clear moonlight, Tycho astride the grandest horse she had ever seen. It was Beauvais's stallion, saved by Tycho from sharing that Knight's cold death. Agnes ran forward, took the boy's outstretched hand and was pulled up behind him. Tycho secured her arms about his waist and kicked his heels.

They hurtled into the forest, Gora vanishing immediately behind them.

Agnieszka was in Kozle within a week, but Tycho let her stay only a few hours. They took Michal and set off before nightfall, beginning a journey that took a month and ended in Gdansk, on the Baltic coast.

They celebrated their freedom in the inns and taverns of the city for several days. Then one evening, while they sat on a stretch of beach looking out at the summer sea, Tycho said that he was leaving. Agnes was not surprised. He had been growing distant, and when she held him, which she did often in the giddiness of her freedom, he had seemed light, a ghost masquerading as a boy.

On the outskirts of Gdansk, along the main road which enters the city from the south, there is a large statue of Saint Sebastien, protector against the plague. It was under this statue that they said goodbye. The sky was grey and overcast, the road beside them growing busy with morning traffic. Tycho, who had made his life from telling stories, was unable to speak. Agnieszka and Michal hugged the boy and then stood in each other's arms as he turned away from them to enter the quiet stream of passing travellers.

He paused once to wave just before he entered the distant forest. The last image they had of him was of a boy with his arm raised steady into the sky.

He turned and became a legend.

Two years passed between the moment of this goodbye and Agnieszka's return to Gora. I believed during this time, much to the frustration of Alex and Krysz and Ahab, that our friends had been recaptured by Pawel's soldiers; captured and secretly buried in some barren field. I believed in Tycho, I largely believed in Ahab and his stars, but I believed more strongly that love was cursed, that any mission on its behalf was doomed.

Then the stories began to trickle into the city.

A traveler would arrive from the west, seek to cure his thirst in one of the alehouses, and surrounded by new friends he would attempt a tale he thought none had heard, that few would believe. Increasingly these travellers spoke of a boy whose stories could bring love to cold hearts, and I knew, for the first time, that Tycho was alive.

Tycho is now known throughout Christendom. He is as famous as was Pawel, as was Jeanne, and his legend describes him as twice born - once by woman, and once by the earth, which swallowed him down into its fiery center to recast him, and then return him to the world as a prophet of love.

I find it difficult to consider my friend a prophet, especially when I recall the nights I spent outside his fur door, but I do consider him a hero, and I am proud of him, as was Ahab. Yet I feel regret as well; a regret that was both relieved and heightened by a letter which arrived in Gora last year.

AUGUST 1434

AHAB

I have been in Paris for several weeks now but am set soon to leave. Last night, while I strolled through the Square before Notre Dame, I overheard two men speaking German, but the one's German was not fluent, and had an accent I recognized.

I introduced myself and learned that he was, as I'd suspected, from Gora. I did not know him but he knew of me; indeed, upon learning my name he grasped me in his arms and begged me to return with him, promising ribbons in the sky, ringing bells, waving arms, and, with a wink, beautiful women.

I declined, regretfully, but have entrusted him with this letter, which I hope finds you, Samuel, and the children, well and at peace.

You have heard, I trust, even in your cold alcove in Gora, the stories about me. A travelling merchant tells a story in an alehouse, it passes from mouth to mouth until it reaches Sam, and Sam, recognizing me as the story's protagonist, brings to you the tale of a boy who wanders about Christendom helping others find love.

You may wonder, why love? How did love become the cause you knew I was lacking?

When Agnieszka and I left Gora we went first to Kozle, but knowing that her home village would not be safe from Pawel's search, we went north to Gdansk. We were travelling with her husband Michal now, and every night, as we prepared to sleep, I lay alone on one side of the fire, and they lay together on the other. A month of summer nights like this, and one of those nights I had a vision.

I dreamt of Agnes and Michal in their old age. I dreamt of them in a high room in the castle. It was summer and I could sense, through the weariness in their sighs and the perspiration on their brows, how powerfully the heat was weighing upon them. They sat on opposite sides of the bed, undressing, their legs reaching towards the floor.

They were so aged. Agnieszka's hair was grey and lifeless; Michal's was gone, and the back of his neck, and his shoulders, were weighed with wrinkles upon wrinkles, little folds of skin hanging near his elbows, under his armpits. Agnieszka's body was spotted with something the colour of tea stains, her breasts sagged, and I could see her ribs shining through her skin.

They were so old and withered, that even waking in the morning, seeing them young before me, I had difficulty shaking this dream of age from my mind. It was a vision almost horrible, and yet I was enthralled. What was it Ahab? What held me so tightly in its hand that I remember that dream now? And feel I will have it with me all my days?

Agnieszka donned a cotton nightdress. Michal rolled onto his back wearing only a thin breechcloth. Without a word, or a wasted movement, they fit themselves together. Michal lay on his back facing the ceiling; Agnieszka lay on her side, facing away from him, her back tucked close against his side.

They fell asleep.

Their feet entwined together.

Her hands pillowed under her cheek, his right hand resting gently on her side. Their breath rising as one in the air above them.

What was it Ahab? What kept those two frail, shrunken, almost unbelievable bodies alive? Why were they not dead and buried? A joint stone marking their grave?

I assumed it was love.

The stories describe me as a prophet of love, but they romanticize me. I know nothing of love. I tell stories, the endings of which I don't know until I've finished, and when I have finished I find that hearts are pounding, hands being taken. I sit silently, ignored now by my audience, and I observe the soft ceremonies of new or awakened love; ignorant as to how I caused these emotions to appear.

I said that I know nothing of love; yet that is not quite true. I know that love is the reason Agnieszka and Michal shall defy time. I know that it is the reason Pawel's last years were ones of misery. I know that love can be a blessing, or a curse, and that this inherent gamble of love's is one that no one will refuse to play, for the alternative, as Sam and I can attest, is to be empty, to have a void in the center of your chest, to feel as though the greatest story of your life is plucked from your soul before it has a chance to be told.

I've told many stories, Ahab. I've never known from where they come, or why they come to me. I don't regret the stories, or the life they've caused me to lead, but I wish I could meet another storyteller someday - a woman of soft voice and gentle touch who will lie me down in the warm grass of a summer field. She'll rest my head in the folds and pleats of her dress and brush her fingers through my hair, her fingertips across my weary eyes.

She'll bid me listen as she tells a story - a love story - and I'll succumb to the soft stirring of her voice, drift away on the waves of her imagination, my own voice, for once, and after all these years, at rest.

Tycho
Paris

1435

If I were wise, and brave enough, I would close this history with a great accounting of the hearts I have herein described. I would weigh the love of Agnieszka and Michal vs the misery of Pawel, attempt to balance Tycho's loneliness against the happiness he brings to others, and perhaps, to be complete, I would also mention the sad deaths of Beauvais and Tonnelli, and Alexandra's decision to waste her love at open windows, expecting them, one day, to offer her the return of the boy she continues to love.

If I had the courage I would do these things, but I know them to lie beyond my power. Perhaps Tycho could weave the garland of words they require, but I shall not attempt them. I shall finish this story as it began; with the one heart I may safely claim to understand.

My name is Samuel. I am a clown who, while writing the history of his friend, has written as well a love story. The story ends well I suppose - the boy finds his mission and the girl returns to her husband. There is joy, but in Tycho's small room, the candles burning about me, I realize that there is sorrow as well; a sorrow which has remained impervious to the changes of recent years.

I once thought that Agnieszka's safe return to Gora, with her husband, would restore my faith in love. I thought that one true and beautiful love story could sweep away the shadows cast by Kristina's death, could restore warmth to my long empty heart. The first few months after Agnieszka's return, if ever so slightly, I did feel a certain rekindling of the spirit, but time passed, as it does so well, and at the age of 36 I can still write that I have never known love in my own life, only its absence. I doubt that this will ever change, and though this once terrified me, it does so no longer. The heart grows numb to pain eventually, and disappointment has little effect upon those who embrace it as the one constant in their lives.

I no longer fear for myself, but still, there are my friends. I pray that Tycho somehow avoids that cold death he predicted for himself. I hope the Lord corrects the cruel fate he imposed upon a teenage boy - giving him a mission, of love, which precludes him from having love in his own life. And Alexandra? I do not know what to wish for her. I wonder at times if it would be better for her to lose her love for Tycho, allowing her heart the freedom to choose someone new. But then there is the risk that she will never love again, she will adopt my life, and surely the pains of unrequited love are preferable to the hollow ache of a chest void of any emotion at all.

I believe that this will be my last night in Tycho's room. I will no longer quit my friends after dinner, wander the halls, and part Tycho's fur door in order to take up my writing. In coming weeks the stains of ink may even fade from my hands. I suppose that I shall need to find a new hobby, something to occupy me, for the future lies ahead like a friend whose conversation I can predict and whose embrace, though sincere, is strangely unsatisfying.

I will grow old in Gora, my age confining me to the castle as securely as did Pawel's unspoken rule. I shall have long conversations with Alexandra. I shall watch Agnieszka raise her family, I shall drink with her husband, teach my tricks to her children.

And I will dream my dreams.

The last few weeks I have dreamt often of running away - shedding the years and complaints of my body to speed off in pursuit of Tycho, finding him in some dark wood. We will share a fire, a rabbit, some stories, and jests. I will accompany him on his journeys and try to save him from his cold death in the snow. It is a simple dream, but it warms me; gives me comfort, when so little else does.

I shall close now. I've spoken enough of things I do not understand. If I am fortunate, this history, the labour of many winter nights, will be unrolled and studied by some scholar in the not so distant future. I hope by then that Tycho's name is legend not only as a teller of stories, but as the founder of a movement. My friend may work miracles, but he is, after all, one boy, and love, it would seem, requires a crusade - a crusade fought with kindness and generosity, and acclaimed by the joyous bells of a thousand city squares: bells which ring out across blue horizons, telling a continent to close its eyes, to dream beautifully, and to awake with hope.

Samuel of Cologne

ABOUT THE AUTHOR

Chris Tomasini is a writer living in Ontario, Canada. He has a long history with the print book – having worked in publishing, bookstores, and libraries. He has studied writing at the University of Toronto School of Continuing Studies, and through the Humber College Correspondence Program in Creative Writing. He is the author of *Festival* – a coming of age novella set in Toronto and London, England. He can be found at christomasini.ca

Manufactured by Amazon.ca
Bolton, ON

27009292R00150